JUST
BUSINESS

Requited Love

MOLLY ALLEN

tellwell

Tellwell Talent
www.tellwell.ca

ISBN
978-1-77962-114-6 (Hardcover)
978-1-77962-113-9 (Paperback)
978-1-77962-115-3 (eBook)

Chapter One

CAITLYN

The scorching sun pierced through my blinds in the early morning grazing across my face already heating it up, I squeezed my eyes together as I felt the pounding in my head hit against my brain. I sat up and stretched my limbs hearing the bones crack into place, I checked the time to see it read 7:45am. I had exactly 60 minutes to get ready and go to work.

It might have been the wrong idea to have a party at a friend's and drink excessively knowing the next day you have work. Even more knowing that today is the day where we have the company CEO coming to work in person for the foreseeable future. Our former manager wasn't meeting guidelines that were set by the company and had to be relieved of duty instantly. Let's just hope this one knows what they are doing and doesn't change how we already run things.

I began to get ready as I did my usual routine and made myself presentable so that I didn't look like a walking corpse. As I moisturise my warm chestnut skin, I noticed the dark bags under my eyes, but a small amount of makeup cleared that up easily. I got dressed in a simple midnight blue pantsuit, grabbed what I needed and left to house to drive to work.

The short drive was still excruciating as my eyes were trying to adjust to the morning blaze. I stopped off for a caffeine boost and to alleviate my hangover and got food to curb the hunger that started to take over my body.

I walked into the building of Black Corporation. The family name of Black has been a large investment in the west side of America as of 20 years ago with the self-made man and Chairman himself John Black making an impact in the hospitality industry. Hearing about his work and that he may have given a co-sign to one of his three daughters, but little is ever heard about them he keeps the information on his private life minimal.

After I signed in I grabbed my tablet seeing as I was the assistant to the previous manager, I had no clue if my position remained intact or if I was to be demoted since they wouldn't know how I worked even though my report says it all.

I looked at my schedule to see that all the department heads were meeting in one of the conference rooms, so I made my way there. I entered and waved to my co-workers and took a seat next to Caleb. Caleb is one of my best friends, my neighbour and the culprit of the party last night.

I have lived next door to Caleb for four years, that's how long I have been living in the small cul-de-sac. He lives with his boyfriend Conor. They are the best gay friends anyone can ask for and took care of me when I first moved in, letting me go to their's for lunch and dinner and taking me to work when I didn't have a car, they were like brothers to me, and I couldn't live without them.

"I'm surprised you even showed up due to how many you guzzled down last night?" he enquired, and I gave him a roll of my eyes and placed my tablet down.

"You should know me better than that, I can manage my drink" I responded as my nose crinkled knowing I was lying.

"You had to get coffee, didn't you?" he asked knowing that I hate coffee in general so for me to even buy it, the hangover was indeed bad.

I turned my body away from him resulting into a quick tickle battle that stopped instantly as we saw the man himself, John Black, enter the conference room. This was a rare occasion as he never came to the building unless it was serious. Might be due to the former manager and who we were to expect next.

The silence could have been cut with a knife, but he made us all ease up as the corners of his mouth curled into a smile and the crow's feet at the edges of his eyes crease deeper.

"I'm sure you are all wondering why I have called you here today, I assume you are aware that your manager will not be returning to work upon gross misconduct at work that we do not tolerate. So moving forward I have appointed the CEO to work here until interviews can be held and we can find someone more permanent for the spot. Until then this is what is the procedure going forward, they will be calling you all in one by one to learn the nature of what you do and your role here to decide on a plan of action" he told us all and we were delighted to have a new boss so quickly and them being a CEO gave us all high hopes that they know the job and will work with us to provide a good business.

"Am I correct that a Caitlyn Pierce is present today?" he asked looking around for a face to a name and I raised my hand as he locked eyes with me, and that same warm smile returned.

"Am I correct that you were assistant to Jared?" he asked, and I nodded letting him continue, "Rest assure your job is stable, and you will be working alongside the CEO still doing your duties" he explained, and I was thankful I still had the best job ever.

With more issues addressed we were all free to leave and return to our respective floor. I made my way into the elevator to head to the top floor where the cubicles were placed for the department heads. There were ten cubicles out on the main floor appointed to each project manager for the departments that we run. Then there was a door that led to the main office for the CEO, the windows were tinted grey, and they had a black trim around them as well as the door with the nameplate of CEO inscribed on a steel plaque.

And then at 6 feet away lay my desk with my named inscribed on my name plaque with the words assistant in small text. I placed my bag down and gathered what I needed to meet this CEO; little did I know what I was getting myself into. I did a quick three knocks before I opened the door and announced myself to not startle them.

"Excuse me, I'm Caitlyn Pierce your assistant I was just-"and all the air was sucked from my lungs as my eyes landed on a very handsome woman sitting behind the desk then she began to stand and approach me.

She was wearing fitted black dress pants and a white shirt with a tie, her sleeves were rolled up to the elbows showcasing some impressive artwork on her forearms. Her hair was dark black and swept back giving full view of her face outlining her soft ivory skin, defined cheeks and jawline but what captured me most were her dark blue eyes. She held out her hand which made me snap out of my trance and I took her hand in mine, and she gave a firm handshake.

"Hello there, Miss Pierce correct?" she asked, and her voice was smooth as velvet.

"You are, but I prefer Caitlyn" I told her as I released her hand as she made her way back around to sit down.

"I mean no offence, but I only call my friends by their first name, you are my subordinate, so I will stick to addressing you as Miss" she said, and I nodded and was a little hurt, but I understood she was in charge and has to keep a boundary between herself and the co-workers.

"As you wish…" and I realised I didn't even get her name as she was finished with the conversation as I was thinking of my words, "I didn't get your name?" I asked and her eyes lightened up and the corner of her mouth quirked up making me regret that I asked.

"I'm Miss Black, it's a pleasure" she said and refocused back on her computer and the realisation dawned on me that this was indeed one of the infamous daughters of John Black. The eyes were the same colour, the height passed down and the features were the same, like father like daughter but a difference in attitude from which I gathered.

"I wish to have your assistance today as I talk with each of the employees, you've been here for a number of years so your knowledge would be valuable" she asked of me and I agreed, there was no need to be getting on her bad side already.

"As you wish Miss Black, just let me know when you are ready and who is first" I told her and gave a nod, and I left the office and only knew I was holding back a breath

5

as I released it as soon as my butt hit my chair and I ran my hand through my hair feeling the stress starting to rest on my shoulders.

She was quick to answer back to me wanting to move forward quickly with each of these talks, as she requested I sat in on each one and as each one concluded, I gave her my best input on the way each person worked and what they brought to the company and how we could possibly improve production. She was impressed with me, giving the fake thinking look with her fingers on her chin but I knew she liked what she was hearing.

Halfway through the day she called for a lunch break which I accepted gladly and left the office main floor already texting Caleb to meet at my car as lunch was my treat. We arrived at a nearby café as we ordered our food and waited with drinks of water.

"So?" he asked as if I knew what he was implying, I raised my eyebrow and he rolled his eyes, "Who is the new CEO?" he asked, and I forgot he didn't have his interview yet and I could spare him the mystery.

"You aren't going to believe this but it's John Black's daughter" I told him, and his eyes widened but I saw the corners of his mouth curl up into a laugh.

"You're kidding me, the eldest?" he asked holding back his laughter for the short question.

"I have no idea, I know he has three daughters, so it could be because that's what businesspeople do, right? They have their oldest inherit the companies" I wondered, I only had knowledge from books I read.

"I mean maybe, only way to find out is to do research, which could be faked information, or ask the source itself" he told me, and I shook my head. There was no way I would get a response let alone even think to ask about her personal life, I just met the damn woman.

"You're thinking too much, maybe some food will help me" I told him as he pursed his lips at me but changed to a wide smile as our food was placed in front of us and we began to eat with some light conversation.

After lunch we made our way back to work and agreed that I would go to his place for dinner tonight which I was fine with, I could not cook anything, I can barely make toast. I got to my floor and continued to attend the interviews with Miss Black.

We worked at a good pace and finished by 3pm and I didn't have long until I was home free, I decided to be risky and thought about Caleb's suggestion and looked to Miss Black as we concluded the last talk, and I was told to leave the office.

"Miss Black?" I began and was already at a loss for words, this cannot go well.

"Yes?" she asked looking impatient waiting for me to speak.

"Are you the oldest of your sisters?" was all I could spit out and instantly regretted what I just asked, I wanted the ground to just swallow me up and not let me out into the world again.

"Miss Pierce let me straighten things out with you right now" she began and turned her chair to face me and in one swift move also turned mine to face her and I froze as her eyes pierced through me.

"You do not ask about my personal life as I do not ask about yours, this is a professional relationship, nothing more and nothing less. Do I make myself clear?" she retorted, and I nodded and shied away, she lifted my chin and raised her eyebrow.

"I said, do I make myself clear?" she asked again sternly, she didn't raise her voice, but she didn't have to for me to understand that she expected an answer.

"Crystal, I apologise for asking that" I said, and she nodded and released my chin and I quickly gathered myself and literally sprinted out of her office not exactly recalling what just happened.

The day ended and I made it out with my life and still having a job, I'd call that a win-win situation and I was glad. I followed behind Caleb on the way home, I pulled into my drive then ran across the grass and entered their home.

The smell of Mexican cuisine filled the home and I only now noticed how hungry I was. I entered their rustic kitchen as I walked to Conor to place a kiss on his cheek to greet him as Caleb walked over after and kissed him.

"How was work?" he asked us both and we told him about our day, but I didn't mention what I asked Miss Black since I didn't want another laughing fit from Caleb again.

"The company CEO is working for us, but Caitlyn is interested in her already" Caleb outed me to Conor, and I was quick to disagree.

"I never said that, it's just not every day you have the daughter of the chairman become your boss" I said, and Conor was surprised by that.

"That's huge, don't mess up" he said, and I rolled my eyes, like I already didn't know that. I have to be cautious and not say something that could ruin my chances of progressing further in the company.

"I won't, I have my charm and I can be a good girl" I teased, and they both laughed as we continue to eat in a comfortable silence and before I knew it I was back home. Resting in my pjs with a glass of wine flicking through different shows to find something to watch. I picked one and then switched to my phone as usual.

I ended up on one of the dating apps I have and was swiping left until a familiar profile caught my attention. In college I had a boyfriend called Damon, and we were together for two years before we called it off, but we stayed casual. I wondered why he was back in the dating scene now. I decided to find out and swiped right and we matched.

I dropped him a text and asked how he was and what was up with the profile, getting a response that didn't confirm my suspicion, he was just hunting for a late night hook up. My curiosity got the better of me and my finger circled the rim of my glass, and I don't know what made me do it, maybe the slight attraction I still had for Damon or maybe it was because it was familiar territory. I sent him a text and stood up starting to pace as my hands got sweaty as I saw the three dots appear and disappear like he was contemplating what I was insinuating.

As I waited and waited I knew what was going to happen as he responded, 'Be there in 10" and now I panicked. Was I really doing this? At least I didn't have to do a walk of shame in the morning.

I cleaned up as fast as possible to not portray as a slob as there was a knock on my door and I opened it to see the familiar man from 7 years ago still looking handsome with his cornrows neatly styled as his dark skin illuminated beneath the porch light and his tall and muscular build towered over me and he gave me a smile.

"I was not expecting this tonight?" he questioned, and neither was I.

"Me neither but here we are" I said and was standing there awkwardly in my baby pink pjs of a tank top and shorts.

"We can just watch a movie if you'd like, we are still friends right?" he asked, and I nodded and thought why I am getting nervous around him.

"You're right, yeah a movie sounds great" I responded we made our way to the lounge and found a movie on tv, and we sat next to each other.

Sitting near each other soon turned into snuggling, then that turned into a simple kiss which started us making out which led to going upstairs to retire for the night. I was going to regret this so much the next morning.

Chapter Two

CAITLYN

I had been up for an hour, fully ready for my day just waiting for the unwanted guest to leave my home. It was another ten minutes before he finally came strutting into the kitchen wearing last night's clothes ready for the walk of shame.

"So, what was that last night?" he asked the corner of his lips curving into the smirk I've now grown to hate.

"Something that isn't going to happen again, I have no idea why it did" I explained to him, turning my back to empty my mug and wash it out. We were old friends that might explain what had happened, but it always became awkward straight after and then I feel guilty for doing that to him. He is a great guy and doesn't deserve to be messed with by the likes of me.

"Whatever you say Caitlyn" he responds, and he doesn't believe me, but I'll prove it to him. I got him to leave by pushing him out the door and rapidly got myself together and then drove to get morning coffee for myself and Miss Black since she texted me her coffee order. This better not be a common request, I have better things to do than be her errand girl.

I got the coffee and made it to work just in time to sign in and make my way up to the top floor. I placed my bag down, knocked on the office door and walked in to see her on the phone in what seemed to be a heated conversation.

Her eyes landed on me and softened which took me by surprise, "I have to go now, I'll call you later" she said and ended the call to whomever it was.

"Is everything okay?" I asked, seeing as it took a toll on her as it was a drastic change from yesterday.

"Yes, thank you for the coffee, you may leave" she said changing back to her cold exterior as I nodded and left the office. I wonder what that call was about that got her so worked up then to just change back to the ice cold bitch she keeps portraying. I believe there is another side to her and I'm willing to take up the task to break the cracks and find it. Even if it risks my career.

I grabbed my tablet and walked to the cubicle where Caleb worked, best thing about my best friend working here is that he is on the same floor as me as he's the head of the leisure department which had him overlooking projects connected to fitness centres as well as gyms. As soon as he noticed me he turned his attention from the computer screen.

"What has you looking so down honeybuns?" he called out to me making me smile at the nickname. I leaned myself against his desk and he turned his chair to face me.

"So, crazy thing happened last night, I hooked up with Damon" I whispered the last part to me, and he didn't look surprised as this was becoming a common occurrence he simply shook his head.

"One of these days, it'll cross the line and you'll be back together" he said, and I shook my head fast.

"No, that will not happen, I'm setting it straight no more crazy hook ups" I reiterated, and he still didn't believe me but who was I kidding, even I didn't believe me.

"I'll believe it when I see it" he said, and I stood up straight as he was about to begin to work again.

"I will, plus I have my sights set on somebody new" I told him as I focused my gaze onto the office where my boss was working away and then my vision was blocked by Caleb's face as he rose to meet my gaze.

"Absolutely not, you cannot be serious to go after your boss" he whispered to me to not let others hear.

"Of course I'm serious, you know me" I told him, but the shakes of his head were making me think I shouldn't do it.

"You're risking your career doing that, it can't happen Caitlyn" he told me, but I simply shrugged and went back to my desk and sat down.

I let the words from Caleb set in, was it worth risking my career for someone I barely know and probably will never know. I don't know what made me want to get to know her, maybe it's because anyone new I meet they take a liking to me, and we become fast friends. Although this time, meeting Miss Black didn't prove that statement, the cold attitude she gives me just makes me want to break it away to find the warm centre.

I was snapped back to reality as a hand snapped their fingers in front of my face and I looked up to see Miss Black as a blush crept onto my cheeks embarrassed from being caught.

"Sorry, what can I do for you?" I asked and grabbed my tablet.

"The amount of time you take to daydream, you could have gotten my task done" she said, and I frowned at her words, why is she so mean to me?

"These files need to be digitalised, I trust you can complete them by lunch hour?" she asked, and I eyed the stacks of files, there was no way I was going to finish by then but the less she knows the better.

"Certainly" I simply said, and she gave me a nod and went back into the office. I ran a hand through my hair and spun once in my chair and looked over to Caleb who shook his head. I gave him a signal to shut up and I began my long day of work.

Lunch hour came sooner than expected and I was only halfway done with the files, but I decided to put my plan into action as Caleb walked over to me.

"Ready for lunch?" he asked, and I grabbed my purse and shook my head.

"You go with the boys today; I got other plans" I told him as my focus was on the office door.

"It was nice working with you" he joked, and I waited until the others left to make my way to the door. I knocked and entered, and she looked up from her computer to meet my eyes.

"Miss Black, would you like to accompany me for lunch?" I asked her and she simply said no and returned her focus back to the screen in front.

"Miss Black it's just lunch, you need to eat and regain your energy and I'm not leaving until you agree" I told her and stood my ground as I crossed my arms across my chest.

"Well then you'll be standing there the rest of your shift" she said, and my mouth dropped open at her rudeness.

"Come on, I'll even pay, you don't even have to leave the office if you don't want to I'll go get it and bring it you back and we can at least eat together" I told her, abandoning the task of leaving the building but still slipping in that I wanted to join her.

She turned and folded her hands in front of her on the desk and raised her eyebrow at me and I gave a small smile seeing as I caught her interest.

"What were you thinking?" she asked, and I gave a full smile knowing I just won.

"Anything you want, burgers and fries or sushi?" I offered two choices knowing they were the closest by.

"Sushi is fine, I'll have whatever you have" she said and looked away and I nodded and left the office in a hurry to not waste more time. Caitlyn 1, Miss Black 0.

It took twenty-five minutes, but I made it back to the office with a bag full of food and drinks as well. I rested it on her desk and emptied out the contents and I may have bought more than I intended to. After it was all out I sat down opposite her and grabbed one of the containers and chopsticks and began to eat.

"You didn't pay too much for all this, did you?" she gave me a curious look as she picked up one of the dishes.

"Like I said, my treat, don't worry about it" I told her as I ate, and she gave a nod and began to eat as well.

We sat in silence for a good ten minutes and I had been contemplating what I could ask her without sounding too eager. I decided to go with the basics.

"So, how long have you worked for your father?" I went with work talk since that's been her focus for two days straight, I thought she was going to be different but she's just like others in charge.

"Since I was 21 years of age" she answered, and I tried to do the math from how old I think she looks. She has a soft face so she must be under the age of 30, no age wrinkles or signs of exhaustion.

"So like, 5 years?" I took a guess and she coughed on her water; I don't think she expected that.

She wiped her mouth and looked at me, her eyes more awake than usual, "I appreciate the flattery" she said, and I shook my head.

"No way you're older than that?" I asked and she nodded her head, and I was now curious, "How old are you exactly?" I asked as I readied myself.

"I'm 33" she simply said, and my eyes widened. I was way off; I couldn't believe there was an eight-year age gap between us both. She obviously had experience in business then.

"I'm 25" I decided to blurt out to not end the conversation.

"I know, I read your file" she told me, and I must have sounded so dumb, but I was curious that she read my file.

"What's in my file exactly, all good I hope?" I asked her, I never knew there were files on everyone here.

"It is, it's why you're in the position you are. You're dedicated to your work, never late, a team player, you could run this business all alone" she said making me blush and I looked down suddenly feeling overwhelmed.

"Thank you" I said, and she smiled at me as I looked up and caught it and she quickly dropped it.

"Have you always lived in California?" I asked her and I placed my empty container down and grabbed my drink.

"Yes I have, in my younger years and teenage years we moved around a lot until my father set down to start his business and I've been here ever since" she told me, and I listened to what she said, this is the longest I've heard her speak and now I'm finally getting somewhere with her. At the mention of her family I saw a small crack in her stony exterior as the softness came back which made me think of the phone call she had received this morning; it was the same look. So that means family phoned this morning and it changed her.

"Sounds complicated" I didn't know how else I could explain it and she looked at me as her expression changed to annoyed and irritated as her eyebrows furrowed together and she stiffened her jaw.

"I wouldn't call it complicated, more like refreshing and pleasant, even though we moved around a lot, we stayed as a... family" she responded but I saw a break at the very end and her gaze grew distant and I cleared my throat and decided to change the subject.

I checked the time and noticed I was going over the hour, "I should get back to work" I told her, and she nodded and agreed quickly.

"You should, I'll clear this up, just go" she said not even looking at me as I quickly left the office knowing I completely messed up. I sat back at my desk and thought of a way to apologise as I began to continue with work.

It was an hour after 5 and I stayed working since I was close to finishing with my task, there was no way I could have gotten this done if I hadn't stayed but once I finally finished and rested back in my chair, I was happy to go home. I switched of the computer and grabbed what I needed as Miss Black also left her office and her gaze focused on me.

She didn't say anything just motioned for me to leave and she followed as we got to the elevator and headed to the ground floor.

"I wanted to say sorry for what happened at lunch, I didn't mean to upset you" I said in a hushed voice, but she heard me as her head turned to my direction.

"Apology accepted, don't let it happen again" she said, and I nodded even though she didn't see me do it. The elevator dinged and we both walked out and then went our opposite ways to head home.

As I got home and did what I needed to do which included ordering food because I still didn't know how to cook for myself, I decided to sit on the couch and look up more about the Black family. I was curious ever since lunch and I couldn't do it at work since she can track our history, I typed in the industry, and found some information about her father but it was mostly private.

I'm aware that she has two sisters, no clue to if they are older or younger, judging by the age of her father and herself, my guess it probably the same age or younger. I don't even know why I'm so interested in her, why must it be my boss of all people.

I wouldn't call it an attraction more like me being intrigued by her. She is handsome though, I noticed today her jawline was so sharp it could cut paper and the way her expressions changed to outline her cheekbones and the way her eyes changed from serious to soft. I quickly closed the laptop from looking at a photo of her and pushed the laptop away, there's no way I just thought of my boss in that way.

The doorbell went off, making me jump but I remembered my food. I answered the door, paid and sat down with my double pepperoni pizza and put on a movie to make me forget what just happened.

I woke up the next morning not ready for work as the thoughts of last night entered my mind, I shook them away quickly as to not think of her in anyway but my boss. I received an email from her explaining that she wouldn't be at work today and sent me what needed to be done. Was it because of my inconsiderate self yesterday or has something else happened?

Chapter Three

RIVER

I took the next day off from work, I was needed at home to be with family. There's a reason we keep to ourselves, a year ago my younger sister Darcy was reported missing. We had no idea what happened to her but with a private investigating team, we managed to find her two weeks later. She was weak, malnourished and barely hanging onto life. We got her all the help possible, but she went mute and didn't speak to anyone about what happened, and we began to fear the worst.

That was until one day I brought a friend over who had similar experiences to Darcy's situation, and I let her go in Darcy's room leaving them for an hour, staying in the room next door. When an hour passed they both came out of the room and for the first time in a while that smile was back on my sister's face. I will never know what they spoke about but just seeing that smile again was enough to know that in time she will be back to herself.

Darcy sometimes has moments where she will lash out for no reason due to a trigger or the nightmares come back to haunt her and over time I became that beacon for her. Just someone she can trust and lean on when she needs.

I pulled up to the family home and took a moment, the anxiety slipping in, but I soon pushed that away as I saw Darcy open the front door. I got out of the car as she ran to me and jumped in my arms.

"I didn't know you were coming; you could have told me" she shouted happily, and I put her down seeing the wide smile and her eyes gleaming with the happiness they hold.

"I wanted it to be a surprise" I told her and wrapped my arm around her shoulder as we walked inside the house. With Darcy being ten years younger than me, I've always been protective off her.

"Well it's definitely a surprise, are you going to be here all day?" she asked a I saw the hope in her eyes, and I didn't want to break it.

"Of course, and I'll sleep over as well so we can have a movie night" I mentioned to her, and she was like a kid in a candy store, the sister I love was always there, just overtaken by a traumatic experience.

"Great, I'll go arrange some movies for us to watch" she told me and ran to the lounge, I smiled as she bounded away, and I made my way into the kitchen to see my mother. The age showing through her grey hair and the stress weighing on her body, but she stays strong for us.

Ever since learning how Darcy became afterwards, being diagnosed with PTSD, anxiety and an eating disorder; my mother thought it best to cut her working hours and stay at home as much as she can. When she can't be here I come, which is the reason I'm here now.

"Thank you for coming on such short notice" she said as soon as she saw me, but I shook my head at her.

"It's never a bother, you go, I got it from here" I told her, she kissed my cheek, and she went to Darcy to say bye and then leave us alone. I began to search the cabinets and fridge to see what food was available that I could make for us later.

"Hey River, what's the plan for dinner?" Darcy called for me and I saw her head pop around the corner.

"Well there's no gourmet dining but we can make a homemade pizza?" I offered and she agreed instantly.

"Definitely and no spinach" she argued, and I raised my eyebrows and held my hands up.

"Sorry for trying to be healthy" I responded back, and she shook her head.

"Pizzas aren't supposed to be healthy" she said and ran back to the lounge, and I made us cocoa and joined her.

We decided on a movie marathon of Keanu Reeves' movies and after the second one I decided to email work to see how things were running.

"Who are you texting, your girlfriend?" Darcy said leaning over to look at my phone.

"No and don't be nosy, it's just work" I told her, and she huffed but kept looking at my phone.

"Whose Miss Pierce?" she asked and began to wiggle her eyebrows to try and tease me.

"She's my assistant and only that" I told her, and she huffed and hit me with a pillow, and I gave her a stoic look.

"Is she cute?" she asked, and I scoffed and rolled my eyes, and she knew I was hiding something, and I was. It's only been a few days and as much as Miss Pierce annoys me, she is cute in her own way, but I would never push anything. I didn't want a label on me, I was there to replace a manager who didn't know boundaries, I wouldn't end up doing the same, I couldn't.

"I'm not answering that" I told her and put my phone away and focused on the movie.

"She is so cute" she teased and poked my cheek making me move away as she continued I broke into a smile which was a victory to her.

As the movie concluded we went to the kitchen to make the pizza. We are both lovers of mushroom so that was our pizza with a tomato base and three types of cheese as well. We also did half spinach for me and the other half pepperoni for Darcy. It didn't look appetising, but we didn't care, we still ate it and enjoyed it. And then for dessert we decided on ice cream and that's when Darcy passed out on the couch.

I carried Darcy to bed and left on her bedside lamp since she is frightened of the dark and left the door open and the hallway light on. As I made my way downstairs and cleaned up, my parents came home from work, my mom coming to me right away.

"How is she?" she asked the worry clear in her voice.

"She's fine, I told you I can manage" I told her, and she relaxed, I saw my father look over as we spoke and then walk away.

"What's up with father?" I asked her and she gave a sigh making me worry for him.

"Just work is stressful, and he received a phone call today but won't tell me who it was" she told me, and I began to get curious. Who would call him and make him act like that, I've always know him to be a good man and never let anything affect him so much except for family so it must be serious.

"He'll tell us when he is ready" I told her, and she nodded as I reassured her the best I could.

"I'm going to go to bed, I have to be up early tomorrow to get back to work as soon as I can" I told her, and she nodded, I gave her a hug and kiss on the head as I headed upstairs to my childhood room and began to get ready to go to sleep.

I was woken up in the middle of the night by Darcy screaming out. I jumped out of bed and ran to her room to see her holding a baseball bat and backed herself into a corner.

I told my parents to move out of the room since I didn't want them to get hurt. I saw the fear in Darcy's eyes, she knew it was us, but something was in her head she couldn't shake. I held up my hands and began to take small steps towards her.

"Darcy, it's me, River" I spoke softly and slowly to her, and I took two steps and I saw her fists clench around the bat, and I stopped moving.

"Please don't hurt me, I did what you asked!" she pleaded with me and right now she didn't see me at all.

"You know who I am, you can put the bat down" I spoke again and did the same motions, and I was about three feet from her, but I saw the look on her face change to anger as the bat came swinging into my side making me drop to my knees. I saw the bat coming for another swing, but I manged to grab it with both my hands before it hit my face and yank it out her hands and throw it out of reach.

She then started with punches and slaps on my chest, but I wrapped my arms around her tightly and tried to calm her down with speaking to her and rocking us back and forth. Thoughts raced through my head, and it broke my heart to know that my parents have dealt with this and have been hurt in the past, but we couldn't do anything. I just kept rocking her against my body and slowly she began to relax as she rested her head against me, and I began to softly sing a lullaby to her in Spanish and soon I heard her breathing slow down as she fell asleep in my arms. I carefully lifted her up and got her back into bed and tucked her back in and this time leaving the light on as I left her room.

I saw my mom in tears and my father holding her. I gave them both a hug and then winced and held my side and my mom got worried.

"I'm fine, she's asleep, if it happens again, I'll go, you two shouldn't have to see that" I told them, and they didn't know what to say as I made my way to the bathroom and locked the door behind me.

I took my shirt off to examine my body and noticed the red tint on my body that will easily form into a bruise by the morning. I looked in the mirror and examined my body, I saw the toned muscle on my body as I took time to look at the tattoos on my arms. Some have no meaning just nice designs and others I'd rather not speak about. I looked to my chest to see the marks from Darcys punches and slaps, I grabbed a cold compress to lay it across my chest, flinching at the coldness.

I cleaned myself the best I could as I put my shirt on and went back to my room, I left the door open and light on and sat on the bed and didn't go back to sleep, afraid of hearing Darcy again.

Morning eventually arrived but I had been downstairs since 5am when I knew she would be okay for now. I was making breakfast for the family, I made strawberry and chocolate chip pancakes, coffee and filled a jug of juice. I set it all out as they came downstairs one by one, and we ate in silence. Darcy had no recollection of last night's events, but I manged to write it down in a journal I kept, I finished eating and looked to Darcy.

"I have to go back to work, but I've called Sasha to come today to take you out" I told her, and she smiled at the mentioned of Sasha. Sasha was the one who I got to come that day to speak to Darcy, Sasha had similar episodes of PTSD and anxiety attacks, so she was the best to help with Darcy. I hated leaving Darcy in this state, but I couldn't be there all the time and she needs help to process all this and I'm not the best for it.

"It sucks you have to go but I get it, but I'm glad Sasha is coming, we'll have fun" she said completely oblivious to the reason why I called in the big guns to help. I finished up and kissed each of their heads, giving Darcy a long hug and then I left to head home to change and go to work.

Chapter Four

RIVER

I walked into work, signed in and made my way to the office checking my phone for any new messages from Darcy or Sasha and only had one from Darcy showing a photo of them both at the zoo. At least she's having fun and is not alone, that's all I care about.

I walked out the elevator into the office space and looked around at each of the cubicles to see them all full and everyone already working. I gave a nod to Caitlyn as I passed by her desk and went into the office and shut the door behind me. I placed my stuff down and sat down in my chair, cue Miss Pierce in 3.. 2… and 1, as if on cue there was the familiar three knocks on the door, she entered the room and I noticed the darkness under her eyes, what was she doing all night? I probably looked the exact same.

"Morning Miss Black, I finished what you asked me yesterday, it's all here" she said and handed me the hard drive where I asked her to file all the reports.

"Miss Pierce, were you up all night working on this?" I asked her and she nodded sheepishly.

"Do you need to go home?" I asked her and she gave me a confused look, probably surprised that I cared, and I do.

I may have a hard exterior, but the health and wellbeing of my employees has always been important to me.

She shook her head rapidly, "No, it's fine I can still work" she said, and I gave an uneasy nod.

"Right well you'll be working in here today, we need to go over documents for the new nightclub we have planned, so can you ask Mr Evans to please come in and we can begin" I told her, and she nodded and left the office.

After this meeting, I'll be sure to make her rest on the couch I have in my office, I can't have her passing out on shift, did she drive here today? I held my thoughts back as they both entered the office and took a seat, and we began with the meeting.

We spoke for an hour about where we want this club based and what features we wanted to be involved. It was my goal to make clubbing become a safe space for people in the future and this was the first step. We made plans to have a meeting with individuals who can make this happen through the construction and financial situation which meant having a business trip but that would be a while away.

As soon as Mr Evans left the room I got up and made my way around the desk to Miss Pierce and took the tablet from her and placed it on the desk and pointed to the couch. She looked up at me with a confused expression.

"Go lay down for an hour or so, you look like you're going to drop at any moment" I ordered her, and she began to open her mouth to protest but I held up my hand to silence her.

"No arguments, go" I told her with authority in my tone as she did as told and laid on the couch, and she instantly closed her eyes and fell into a deep sleep. I smiled at how tired she must be. I didn't want her to burn herself out with work, I told her to work but it didn't bother me if she didn't finish it. I sat back down on my desk and grabbed her file to take another read.

Caitlyn Marguerite Pierce, 25 years of age, grew up in San Diego but moved here when she was 18 to attend university. Diligent worker, dependant and a team player when it comes to the company. Worked here for four years and made assistant after only two years for making the company gain one million in six months through a fast-paced investment strategy. That was her? I heard about that, but I wasn't told who made that happen. She really is something, I looked over to her and watched how she slept.

The shallow breaths she took and the way she folded her hands under her head and those soft lips. I shook my head and quickly closed the file and stuffed it into a drawer. That didn't just happen, I quickly got up and decided to go and get lunch for us both, she'll sure be hungry when she wakes up.

I made my way out to grab food she might enjoy, she did mention burgers the other day, so I decided on that and just got cola since I saw a bottle on her desk the first day I came here. I got back to see her still asleep, I laid out all the food and walked over to her and gently shook her awake. She opened her eyes slowly and got startled to see me that close to her, she shot up into a sitting position as I backed away and held my hands up.

"It's only me, I was wondering if you were hungry, I got you food" I told her as confusion and surprise spread across her face as she looked to the desk to see that I wasn't lying. I walked over to the desk and removed my jacket to roll my sleeves up and sat down as she sat opposite me still in a state of paralysis from waking.

"Thank you for the food" she says finally getting back to her normal self as she began to eat, and I could tell she was thankful for it.

"You're welcome, you seem better now you've slept" I told her, and I bit down into my burger.

"It wasn't much but it'll do" she said, and I didn't mind sending her home early, truth be told I didn't see her car parked in the usual spot so she must have gotten a lift today. If she lasts till end of work, I'll drive her home myself.

We ate in silence, and I could tell she was battling with her inner demons as her face kept changing expressions, but I had no idea what she was thinking. After we ate and I disposed of the trash she got up to leave then turned to me and I waited for her to speak.

"Permission to speak of the record?" she asked me, and I raised my eyebrow at her and placed my hands inside my pockets.

"Excuse you?" I retorted, confused by what she meant.

"Permission to speak to you like you aren't my boss for a moment?" she asked again and never once have I been asked this, and I was slightly intrigued by what she had to say so I gave her a nod to continue.

"Is the reason you didn't come to work yesterday because of what I mentioned when you spoke about yourself?" she asked and I couldn't believe this girl, so self-centred.

"Believe it or not *Miss Pierce* the world does not revolve around you, people do have their own issues and lives going on" I told her and the anger that coursed through her was fast.

"I understand that but do not talk down to me like I'm some idiot, it was just after the phone call in the morning to our talk you seemed off" she said and was starting to raise her voice and I knew people in the next room would hear.

"And I have a right to keep my life private, I do not have to explain anything to you" I said now walking closer to lower our voices, but I kept a strong stance.

"Then what was with the work load you threw at me yesterday and through a damn email, you can call you know?" she responded back, and I couldn't understand why she was getting so annoyed at me.

"It was a simple work request; I didn't expect it to be done in one day" I told her, and she ran a hand through her hair and rolled her eyes and I waited for her response.

"Because you didn't tell me a time limit, how am I supposed to know when you don't talk to me!" she raised her voice at this point, and I had to end this conversation before people start talking.

"Now Miss Pierce, like it or not I don't have to be nice to everyone, now since this is off the record, how about you shut your mouth before the entire floor hears this" I told her, and she just smirked at me and I didn't expect her quick response as she got up close and personal.

"How about you shut it for me?" she said, and her eyes widened as did mine as she also parted her lips completely taken back by what she just said as my eyes followed her own and then took a glance to her lips, but I withdrew myself and took a step back.

"I suggest you leave" I told her, and she quickly regained where she was. She just nodded and quickly left the office.

Where did that come from? I knew she gained a fondness for me, but surely it didn't reach past that to attraction. She knows that can't happen, a man just got fired for gross misconduct and if that happened to me, it would ruin the family name. I couldn't believe I was thinking if it happened and the consequences of it. It can't happen and it won't, I have to make sure of that.

I let a reasonable amount of time pass before I grabbed her tablet and opened the office as all the others who worked here quickly looked away as I walked out. I passed her tablet to her, and she didn't even look at me.

"If you need to go home early, you can do, you won't be losing any pay" I told her, and she just nodded still not looking up. I walked around to the side of her desk where the others wouldn't see what I was about to do.

I grabbed her chin and turned her head to look at me as her mouth hung open and eyes widened.

"I expect when I talk to you in the future, you make eye contact with me, do I make myself clear Miss Pierce" I leaned down and whispered to her, and she slowly nodded.

"I'm sorry?" I asked and gripped tighter wanting her to use her words and not just give me motions.

"Yes Miss Black" she croaked out and I released her chin and she started to grab her stuff to leave as I entered my office and closed the door and smiled to myself. I had power over her, I won't abuse it, but it might be fun to make her squirm from time to time, punishment for speaking to me like that.

I did more write ups on documents needed in the coming months and by the time I finished it was 5pm, so I grabbed my briefcase and jacket and left the office as I saw everybody else leaving. I looked to Caitlyn's desk and noticed a crumpled piece of paper; I waited till everyone was gone as I grabbed it and opened the piece of paper.

It was just a bunch of drawn hearts and a pair of lips; I shook my head and threw it in the nearby trashcan and made my way out to the elevator. I got to ground floor and nodded to the janitor as I left the building and drove home.

I parked in the garage and made my way inside, I've always hated living in a large home all by myself, it always felt lonely. It'd be nice to have Darcy come live with me, but I doubt she is ready for that.

I went to the kitchen and poured myself a small glass of whiskey as I downed it in one and then poured another. I couldn't believe how this week was going. I get moved to a new company completely lost on what is happening with no notice. I went back home to take care of my sister which isn't a burden I just want her to get well in her own time and then only today Caitlyn basically asked me to kiss her.

I drank the whiskey and needed to shower to drown away all the negativity that happened so far. I had to get her out of my head, and I'd do everything possible to shake away that feeling.

Feeling refreshed I went to the kitchen and made myself a quick meal, went to the lounge and sat down to watch something as I ate. I need a roommate or something, it's so quiet. Even if I get Darcy to live here maybe I could ask Sasha as well, there's two spare rooms so that wouldn't be so bad and the days I can't be here, I'm sure Sasha wouldn't mind since her work is remote.

It was an idea to ask them in the morning, I just needed tonight to reset my brain and not think about work or-

My phoned signalled a text and I grabbed it to see Caitlyn's name flash then vanish, I opened the text chat and she had sent me a message then removed it. I quirked an eyebrow and waited to see if she would send anything as the three dots kept appearing then disappearing and then she eventually went offline.

Well that ends that, I wonder what she put? Must have been about what happened in the office and that was the wrong think to start thinking about. I finished eating and lay on the couch as I used this as a distraction to watch tv and hopefully fall asleep and dream of this show and not a certain dark-haired beauty.

The next few weeks consisted of various meetings for the new project as well as glances between Caitlyn and I and small little remarks to each other. I couldn't let it go that easily, I enjoyed it, it brought a sense of danger and riskiness to try and hide at work and the blouse she wore with the first few buttons undone did not go unnoticed and I soon called her to my office.

She walked in and took a seat in front of me as she started fidgeting with her fingers and biting her lip in a nervous fashion.

"Is this about spilling coffee on the documents, I backed up the files it's easy enough to reprint them?" she rapidly said, and I didn't even knew that had happened. I raised my eyebrow.

"You did what?" I asked but she closed her mouth.

"Never mind" she simply said and motioned for me to tell her what this is all about.

"We have a business trip to San Francisco in the coming weeks and I would like you by my side during the meetings?" I asked her and her cheeks flushed knowing that I considered her company.

"Wouldn't Mr Evans be better since it's his department?" she asked, and I smiled at her, and she got more confused.

"He will be attending of course, but you will be coming to help me out, so will you?" I asked again and she nodded her head clearly still not getting her head around it.

"Yes, of course, it'll be my pleasure" she said and began to get up to leave and I wasn't done yet.

"Miss Pierce?" I called her and she turned to face me, "Please button up the rest of your shirt, you're causing a distraction" I teased her, and the blush grew deeper on her cheeks, and she quickly buttoned them up and left the office. I was going to enjoy this business trip; it couldn't come sooner.

Chapter Five

CAITLYN

It has been two months since Miss Black came and joined our company and to say it has been complicated would be an understatement. It's like she had split personalities. One day she'd be nice and kind and seems like she wanted to be friends and get closer, then the next day completely closed off and reverting to the ice queen persona.

Even the other employees would notice the changes in her exterior and began to get worried that something bigger was happening, but no one had the courage to ask if she was okay, they relied on me asking instead.

At times I would ask and just be shrugged off or just get the same answer of her being fine and I had to deal with that to not push her to a limit.

But weeks went by like this, and it only really changed the week leading up to the business trip where she seemed agitated and then changing to being happy and excited. It was confusing and I didn't know what day it would be good or not.

We took a plane to San Francisco, and I decided on sleeping through the journey after not sleeping the last two nights from being too excited and overworked for what this trip would entail. The most I know is that where we were staying was a five-star hotel since Miss Black only opted for the best. Michael the head of the department that came with us was staying in his own room and the only one left was two rooms that were adjoined, and I didn't mind that as it was a way to be close to her.

I asked why we weren't having a penthouse suite or something extravagant like that and her answer was that she didn't want to spoil us or make us get used to the riches, but I think it was deeper than that.

We got a taxi to the hotel, got the keycards and headed to our rooms to settle in after which we would be going out for dinner in the evening with executives for the project. I unpacked my bag and then opened the balcony doors to enjoy the bustling city streets of San Francisco as a knock came from the door that joined our room.

"Come in" I called out as I turned around to see Miss Black pop her head in.

"Is the room to your liking?" she asked, and I saw her hands clasped in front of her and looking sheepish.

"It is yes, can I ask why you got adjoining rooms for us?" I asked her as I stepped more into the room.

"Just so I know where you are at all times and keep an eye on you" she said and gave me a smile which I returned.

"Well it's perfect, thank you Miss Black" I said, and she raised her hand to scratch the nape of her neck.

"Caitlyn, we have known each other for two months now, I think out of the office you can call me by my first name" she told me, and I grew nervous suddenly and didn't expect her to open to me a little more and even knowing her name was a huge step from how closed off she used to be.

"I would if you had given it me?" I questioned and it just hit her, and she became embarrassed as her cheeks flushed colour.

"Right yes, my name is River" she told me, and I smiled finally hearing it.

"River Black, it suits you" I told her, and I gave a smile which she reciprocated.

"Well, I'll be in here, dinner is at 7 so make sure you're on time, dress code is semi-formal" she said and went back into her room and closed the door.

Hopefully these few days will prove to be worth it, for the main project at hand and my own little one I have in progress. The three of us got together to go over what would be explained in the meeting and a little about the other executives there and then we had to leave to go get ourselves ready.

It was a lot, but we managed to understand it easily, and my plan was just to let these two speak since I still don't understand why I was here, but I wasn't going to complain about it.

I left to my room to shower and pamper and prepare myself for the meeting. I opted on wearing a long off the shoulder v cut black dress with a slit going up to mid-thigh. I curled my hair and applied light make up to hide the fatigue that had been building up over the last few days from working and over thinking.

As I finished putting on my silver strappy heels, I heard a knock on the door, and I grabbed my clutch bag and opened the door. Michael was wearing grey coloured dress pants, black loafers, a black shirt and his jacket held in one hand. He cleaned up well and his hair was styled to give a more executive look by the amount of gel he used gave a shine to it.

Then my eyes shifted to River and my breath got caught in my throat. I've seen her in suits all the time at work but this time she wore the simple black suit and white shirt but instead had the top three buttons undone, and I didn't expect her to do that from her number of complaints of my choice of clothing in the office. Her hair was styled neatly into the usual quaff, and I also noticed a very small amount of makeup. As her eyes stood out more due to mascara and eyeliner and her lips also seemed more eye-catching from being outlined with lip liner and I was starstruck by how handsome she looked.

"You look great, shall we?" Michael said and motioned to let me walk first, I nodded and closed my door and led the way out of the hotel and into the limo that was requested for us.

I eyed River on the drive there otherwise Michael held my attention with unimportant questions. She still hadn't said a word or even looked at me, I started to get worried and then the car came to stop, and I had my chance.

"Michael you head on in and save us a seat, I just want to go over a few things with Miss Black as her assistant" I told him, and he seemed none the wiser and closed the door behind him and headed inside. River was also about to leave but I grabbed her wrist to stop her, and she sat back slowly.

I waited a moment to see if now that we were alone she would say anything but still silence and no eye contact and I began to feel like I was too overdressed, or the dress just didn't suit me.

"River you haven't looked at me or said one word since I left my hotel room. Am I over dressed for something like this or is it not suitable?" I began to fear and over think too much but then her eyes met mine and I stopped talking as I watched as she took in my entire being. She smiled as her eyes checked every inch of me and I began to feel insecure as no one has ever studied me like she just did.

"You're perfect" she whispered, and my jaw dropped as she gazed into my eyes, and I was left speechless. "You're beautiful" she continued, and I couldn't think of anything to say but the heat on my cheeks increased in intensity, I began to look away from feeling self-conscious, but her hand grabbed my chin to make me look at her and this is my newfound feeling of being submissive to her demands.

"Don't shy away from me" she whispered and began to lean in, and my eyes closed as if on command but a knock on the window made her pull away from me like I was the plague and I deflated.

She got out the car first to see who interrupted us and I felt my cheeks and tried to relax myself and then I heard her clear her throat and hold her hand out to me. So I took her hand and got out of the car and the breeze in the cold evening air made me relax instantly as it was the driver who interrupted us.

River told them a time to come back for us and she opened the door to the restaurant for me and I entered as she followed. We found our table with ease as Michael saved us two seats and I was glad to sit next to River. There were eight other men here all older than me from the years of experience through the grey hair they had and the wrinkles in their faces and hands. Then there were two women as well who gave River and I warm smiles probably feeling more comfortable other women were here. I often seem to forget that River is from a formidable family and people know her well if they work in the industry.

The meeting started up easily with introductions and then getting straight into business as papers and documents were passed around and I was just watching every movement and taking in every word each other were saying. This is my best way to learn, and I picked it up quite easily and as River was passed a documented file and went through it, I leaned over and looked. She moved to share it between us both and then gave me an expecting look.

"What do you think?" she asked in a hushed voice as she passed me the entire file and I went through it more thoroughly and began to pick up on certain deals that didn't make sense, or they were asking for too much.

I looked at the man opposite us and he was already watching, he gave me a disgusting smirk as he drank his whiskey and took a long inhale of his cigar and slowly blew the smoke out as I waved my hand to dissolve the fumes. With the dark hair he tried to keep but the grey showing through, he didn't look as old as the other men here he seemed to be in his late 40's but something seemed so familiar to me.

"80/20 split, assuming that we get the 80?" I asked the man in front of me, and he gave a hearty laugh and leaned forward as he rested his hands in front of him.

"Little girl, this is where the adults play, you don't deserve the 80" he said and looked to his team next to him and they just nodded to him but not looking at me.

"I'm sorry but that won't satisfy us. You wouldn't even be getting a project without Miss Blacks idea, so I suggest you stop acting like an all-mighty corporative imbecile and rethink your offer, please excuse me" I insisted and grabbed my bag and got up and made my way to the restroom.

How can one man act so arrogant, I hate people like that. I just came here to cool off, I walked over to the sinks and washed my hands and topped up my makeup as the other two women from the table walked in.

"You've caused an argument out there" Jessica, I remembered her name, told me and I gave her a look as she stood at the sink on the right side of me as the other woman Layla stood on my left.

"What do you mean?" I asked her and we all did our makeup taking our time.

"They don't know why you spoke, but your boss is sticking up for you the best they can" Layla informed me, and I smiled at knowing I wasn't just pushed aside.

"I'll tell you now; you got balls for saying it like it is to Mr Huntington" she said, and my head snapped to her from hearing that name which I haven't heard in eight years.

"I'm sorry, did you just say Huntington?" I asked again and she gave a nod. I felt an old sickening feeling settle in my stomach as I grabbed my purse and left the restroom and quickly made my way to River. I grabbed her arm and she quickly got up to look at me.

"I have to go" I quickly said, and she began to worry for me as she looked me over.

"Are you okay?" she asked but I shook my head and kept insisting to leave.

"I just have to go, I'm sorry" I said and didn't even look back as I bolted towards the door and left and began to breathe heavily and I couldn't catch my breath.

That name, that face, that smile. I remember him, I remember his son, I remember it all.

It happened eight years ago, I was in high school the typical cheer captain and at the time dating the basketball captain Ethan Huntington. We were the power couple of the school and dated from sophomore year to end of junior year. I was invited to his house just like any normal couples would do and thought nothing different of it. He informed me his dad was home and I never met his dad as I was told he was always out on trips or stuck at work, so it was time to meet him.

Reginald Huntington I learnt who his father was and at the start he was a very nice man, he was kind and gave us space when we were around. But one day I went to the house as Ethan had texted saying to come over, but he wasn't there, and I didn't know until I got there but his father was. I was let in and was allowed to wait so I went to the lounge and watched TV while I waited.

I felt a bit out of place and my brain was telling me to keep on guard and to just get out of there, but I was 17 and I froze out of fear. Reginald had sat down next to me very closely and spoke to me like anyone else would but then started asking very uncomfortable questions. What I did in my own time for pleasure? My bra cup size? What colour underwear I wore? I just laughed it off and tried to move away until he put his arm around me, the scent of cigarettes and whiskey filled my nostrils and made me sick, but I was trapped by this large man. He leaned in and started to sniff my hair as he placed his hand on my thigh and started to move it up my skirt. I freaked out, I couldn't move and was fearing the worst, but the front door was heard, and he removed his hands and stood up like nothing happened as I sat there disgusted with myself.

When Ethan came back his father just told him a fabricated story to hide what he just did. A week later I broke up with Ethan as it happened for another week and got worse. I never reported it and now I wish I did.

Two hands grabbed my face and pulled me back to reality as a pair of deep blue eyes gazed into my hazel ones and her mouth was moving but I couldn't hear as the beating in my chest was getting worse. She sat me down on the ground and my hearing finally popped back into existence as I heard her words.

"Deep breathes okay, just follow with me" she said and began to take breathes in and out and I couldn't control it at first but got into sync as I regained my breath. She took of her jacket and wrapped it around my shoulders as Michael came over with a bottle of water which River took from him and gave it to me to drink. I never took my eyes of River feeling a sense of safety with her.

She got out her phone and called for the limo to come for us now when she hung up she kept her focus on me, and I appreciated it. Once the limo arrived she helped me up and into the limo and we drove back to the hotel. Neither one of them asked questions and I was thankful for that, I felt so embarrassed from the scene I caused and probably messed up the business deal as well.

When we got back Michael went to his room as River helped me into mine. She sat me down on the bed as I didn't have much energy or spoke at all, but she was patient with me. She leaned down in front of me as she undid my heels and took them off my feet and placed them to the side. She stood up and cautiously moved closer to me and removed my earrings and placed them on the dresser then grabbed makeup wipes and came back and carefully wiped my face.

As she came to my lips and carefully rubbed the lipstick off my lips, her thumb replaced the wipe. She stroked across my lips, and I turned my head to face her, and she didn't move or back away from me as her hand moved to cup my cheek.

She was about to speak but I leaned in and let my lips hit hers. She froze up and I began to realise what I just did as my cold lips met her warm ones, but I soon felt warmth as she kissed back but it didn't last long as she pulled away and got up.

"I'll order us some food; you should get changed and wash up" she said and left through the door joining our rooms. I would have felt embarrassed or empty if it wasn't for the crimson colour I saw on her cheeks and the smile as she spoke to me. I sat there still in a daze until I realised what she asked of me and began to regain control of my body.

I went to the bathroom and looked in the mirror to see the matching colour on my cheeks and the smile stuck on my face and light back in my eyes. I knew I had to explain myself for what happened but right now I was thankful for how she took care of me and didn't pressure me at all. I felt safe with River. I felt like I could trust River. I was falling for River.

Chapter Six

CAITLYN

I got dressed into my pjs and wrapped a blanket around myself and sat on my bed with my legs curled up. I was scrolling through my phone when River knocked on the door and came back in, also looking different as her make-up was removed and she was wearing grey sweatpants and a simple black t-shirt. She sat on the chair opposite the bed and looked at me and her face softened.

"Are you okay?" she asks, and I sat up and crossed my legs.

"I'd rather not talk about it" I told her, and she nodded, understanding that I needed time to wrap my head around it.

"I'm sorry if I ruined the business deal" I told her, I felt bad because what if we don't get this chance again.

"Don't be sorry, we can find other people who would want to be involved, but you were right 80/20 was not right" she said, and I smiled knowing that I helped there.

"I'm also sorry for not asking if I could kiss you" I said my voice going into a whisper since it felt embarrassing to bring it up.

"So, you're sorry for not asking but not sorry for doing it?" she asked as her eyebrow raised up and I felt the blush come back again.

"I'm 100 percent sure I don't regret doing it but still it wasn't right" I told her, and she nodded as there was a knock at the door and she went to go get our food.

I am honoured that she hasn't left me and is staying with me to make sure I'm okay. This softer side of her is what I'm starting to like, she must have younger sisters for her to be like this with me, the protective and kinder side, I just hope it lasts.

As we ate she told me that we have another day here but then we leave at night. I felt bad because I wanted it to just be us two, but I knew Michael was also here, that ruined the mood, and I knew we couldn't act like we were now.

"So, you have a younger sister?" I asked looking down at my plate, I decided to try and get to know her better and to also prove my theory correct.

"I do yes, she's ten years younger than me so I care for her dearly" she said, and I looked up at her and nodded. Her sister is near my age, but I know she has another sister as well.

"And what about your other sister, I know you have two, is she also younger or not?" I asked and I saw the look on her face change to a more distant look and it was bringing back memories from the first week we met.

"Uh yeah, she is older than me by 2 years, but we don't really talk anymore" she says, and I can see a look of regret hidden in her eyes, but I kept pushing like the nosy person I am.

"Why not?" I asked and she shook her head and stood up.

"It's getting late, you should sleep" she says and doesn't say anything else and just goes to her room. Well done me for ruining something again.

Why do I have to keep pushing? I can't even count how many times I have done that; I need to learn to keep my mouth shut and not involve myself in other people's lives.

The next day was not even going the way I planned and not because Michael joined us but because River has gone back to the ice-cold bitch we know and hate. I was glad Michael was here though because it didn't create awkward moments and I could just talk to him, turns out he is great company and has a very likeable personality.

We stopped to get lunch and he paid for us and waited in line, leaving River and I waiting. I looked at her, but her eyes were trained on looking out the window.

"You can't ignore me forever River, we work together" I whisper yelled at her and she turned to look at me.

"That is all we will be" she tells me, and I grew confused at that, there's no way I'm back tracking not with how far I've got.

"What do you mean by that?" I asked her and she leaned forward to not raise attention to us.

"It means, no more asking about my personal life I and I won't do the same with you, do you understand?" she asks, and I nodded to her.

"I guess so" I whispered, and Michael came back with drinks.

"So what did I miss?" he asks, and we both remained silent, and he got the gist to not ask questions.

We ate in complete silence, and it was frustrating, the walk back to the hotel was as well and as River went to her room she slammed the door shut, how childish.

"Is Miss Black okay?" Michael asked and I forgot he was out the loop.

"I honestly don't know but thanks for paying for lunch, I owe you at work one day" I told him, and he smiled and waved it off then went to his room as I went to mine.

I began to pack my bag knowing we would be leaving soon and go back to work like none of this had happened. I was so close to breaking that exterior, but I just had to run my mouth like usual, I grabbed my laptop and began to do another deep search on the notorious Black family.

I went through different sites and articles just to find anything about her, her sisters just anything I could gather to understand it all better. But anything that seemed like something ended up being nothing. I pushed my laptop to the side and gave up on the search. I hope in time we can fix whatever this is, and I can just ask and find out that way. I can't believe what people say as it may just be a rumour.

We left in the evening, the quietest journey ever and when we touched ground it was just a set direction to get us all home and safe and nothing else said. If she acted different at work too, I didn't know how much more I could take of it.

I walked into work the next day, the anxiety growing in the pit of my stomach as I knocked and walked into the office to see her here like usual. The familiar setting came back from when we first met, she wasn't even looking at me.

"River?" I called for her and she looked up with confusion on her face.

"I'm sorry, you did not just call me by my first name, we are at work now Miss Pierce so please refrain from friendly interactions" she tells me and my whole world just dropped hearing those words. I knew it would be different, I just had to think it.

"Are you fucking serious right now?" I shouted at her, I was done with this bullshit, and I am not coming to work to be tossed around back and forth just for her to make fun of me.

"Excuse me, I don't need to remind you again" she tells me and gets up trying to intimidate me, but I was not going to back down to the likes of her.

"No, I'm done with this shit, stop treating me differently every single day, I can't take the mixed signals" I practically begged as I felt the tears starting to brim in my eyes, I didn't want to cry in front of her, but it will happen.

"I don't know what you want from me?" she asked and that's the first real sentence I have heard from her as her voice laced with want, a want that I wasn't even sure if I can provide that.

"Just to know you better than what I get told or what you tell me, why won't you open up to me?" I asked her as I wiped the first tear that fell.

"Because… I don't have to" she said and that was it, I wasn't going to stand around and hear this anymore.

"Then fuck you" I said and just left the office. I was over it, if she only saw me as an assistant then that is what she will get.

The next couple of days it was painful to keep up the façade that I didn't want to be close, but I had to remain strong. I noticed though that she tried to keep me talking for longer by asking questions that she already asked or tried to ask about my day, but I ignored her for the majority and gave her the same treatment that she gave me.

I made my way to the photocopying room to get document copies for the next meeting with all the head of departments to see what projects everyone is working on and if they need help or to continue forward for the next phase. I heard the door open and then another presence was in the room, I looked over my shoulder to see River, I quickly looked away and focused on printing.

"Are you planning on trapping me in here Miss Black?" I asked her without looking at her, I felt the tension in the room grow thicker as I felt her move around the space as she leaned against a table to my right as I saw her out the corner of my eye.

"No, I actually need to photocopy something" she said, and I just nodded as I waited for this machine to hurry up since I didn't want to keep talking. Then to my luck the machine stopped working.

"You have got to be fucking kidding me?" I said and kicked the machine as River got up and made me stop.

"That isn't going to help, let me have a look" she said and began to dismantle the thing to get into the centre.

"Do you actually know how to fix it or are you just trying to get me to talk to you?" I asked her and she looked at me with her cold expression and I knew then to be quiet.

"I actually do know how to fix it" she said and began to do what was necessary. I had nothing else to do so I just waited and watched. And I couldn't help myself, I watched how her arms flexed under her shirt and then at the forearms, I was thankful she always rolled her sleeves up.

I noticed a date that was tattooed on her arm, 04/20/09. What happened in 2009? Thoughts ran through my head, but I reminded myself not to ask as it was already awkward, and I didn't want to make it worse.

I heard the machine come alive again as she fixed it and placed the last piece in place and removed the jammed paper that was in it but as I moved forward to continue she blocked me. I froze and just kept my eyes on her chest that was heaving with her heavy breaths, and I didn't know what to do. She lifted my chin with quite a good grip, and I felt my mouth part as she gazed into my eyes.

"If you ever swear at me again, I'll make you regret ever remaining to be my assistant" she said, and I quickly nodded, and she brought me closer to her, smirked and I saw her tongue lick her lips slowly and I blinked.

"Yes Miss Black" I said, she was satisfied and released my chin and moved out the way. As soon as I copied the documents, I ran out of that room. Who the heck does she think she is? I was outraged, the mixed feelings again, I've had enough. I went back up to the floor and went to the conference room and laid out the documents and just waited there as I couldn't be anywhere near her right now.

The meeting started and we ran through everyone's current projects, after Caleb spoke he gave me a concerned look, but I shook my head to not worry him, I know he'll ask later. We mentioned the nightclub project again and I was thankful that we have other executives interested and I excused myself and left the room.

I began to feel sick as the constrictions in my chest came back and I saw Caleb leave the room to come check on me. He quickly came to me and placed his hands directly on my cheeks.

"Okay relax, deep breaths" I began to do that to avoid the panic attack I felt coming, then I just buried my head against his chest, and he walked me back to my desk and sat me down and kneeled next to me.

"What's going on?" he asked, and I remember I didn't even tell him, but he and Conor know about my past and I knew I could trust them.

"On the business trip, I saw Ethan's dad, Reginald and it brought so many memories back and I had a panic attack, and I just haven't had the chance to figure it out or talk to someone yet" I told him, and he rubbed my arm and grabbed his phone.

"Look, I'm going to call Conor to come get you, don't worry about Miss Black, I'll deal with her, you need to go home" he said, and I didn't argue with him, and I let him make the call as he gathered my things and walked me down to the ground floor as we waited for Conor to take me home.

I got home and Conor told me that he and Caleb will come check on me when they finish work and I just nodded and made my way inside, there's only one person I knew I could talk to more about this, Damon.

Although we didn't start dating until college, Ethan attended the same one and when I told Damon about my past, he found Ethan and beat the crap out of him. I didn't condone violence and it wasn't even Ethan who did anything but in that moment, Damon saw him as the next best thing since he didn't know his dad.

I called Damon to come over and he did thinking I was asking for a hook up as he entered my home.

"I knew you'd call soon" he said, and I rolled my eyes and shook my head.

"This isn't what you think it is, I just need you as a friend right now, can you be that for me?" I asked and he knew I was serious as the tears welled in my eyes and his demeanour dropped to the caring man I know.

"What happened Caitlyn?" he asked as I sat on the couch, and he came to sit next to me and wrapped an arm around me.

I told him everything, about work with Miss Black, the business trip and about Reginald and I felt the anger radiate off of Damon, but I kept him calm to not go out and cause chaos.

"You have to call the police about this" he said, and I shook my head and stood up.

"They won't do anything, I'm eight years too late" I told him, and he stood as well.

"You were a minor Caitlyn, it's fucking bad!" he yelled at me, and he knew I could go one decibel higher than him.

"I know that Damon, you don't have to remind me, but little I know he has a shit ton of lawyers that will bail him out in no time!" I yelled back and he backed down instantly.

"So what do you want to do?" he asked, and I ran a hand through my hair trying to think.

"Not think about it, I will get help, I promise but even talking to you about it is helping" I told him, and he nodded.

"I'm still your friend, I'll always be here for you" he told me, and I was thankful that he was still a good friend that I had. Later on Caleb and Conor joined us to make sure I was okay. I spent the night at Conor and Caleb's home, as I did not feel like being alone and they even allowed Damon to stay over as well as they told him to take me to work as they have an appointment and Caleb couldn't take me.

Chapter Seven

RIVER

I woke up feeling like my head was going to explode. I didn't sleep at all as I had Caitlyn running through my head since Caleb told me she went home. I hope she is okay; it must be about what happened on the trip since she left after that was announced.

I wonder what had happened, it had something to do with Reginald Huntington. She has never worked in any other company apart from this one, so it wasn't work related, maybe education, but he was never a teacher. I tried to pinpoint what it could be related to then I remembered I shouldn't even be doing this. I set her straight to not ask me about my life if I didn't with hers but why am I so drawn to her?

I managed to get showered and dressed for the day and before I left I gave a call to Darcy to see how she was. I made breakfast as I left it on speaker when she picked up.

"River I was sleeping, it's too early to speak" she groaned, and I knew she hated waking up so early.

"I'm sorry, I just wanted to ask you something very important" I told her trying to get her interested and I heard movement on the other side.

"It better be important so I can go back to sleep" she says, and I figured after I tell her what I have planned she won't go back to sleep.

"So, I have been talking with mom and dad over the last few weeks and they have allowed me to have you move in with me, if you want?" I asked and I was glad she was on speaker as the biggest squeal was heard.

"Are you serious, please tell me you are not messing with me right now?" she shouted down the phone to me and I smiled to myself, happy to hear her excitement.

"Of course, but only on one condition?" I told her and she stayed quiet to let me continue. "Sasha also has to move in" I told her, and she was still happy, and I was glad she was close with Sasha.

"Of course, oh my gosh, this is the best surprise ever, when can I move in?" she asked, and I looked at the dates when I know Sasha is free.

"About three days and Sasha will come over as will I and we'll help you pack and get you moved in" I told her, and she squealed again.

"This is the greatest day ever, thank you River, I love you so much" she said, and I could hear her try and hold the tears back.

"I love you too Darcy, now go back to sleep" I told her, and I heard her scoff on the other side making me laugh.

"Yeah right, I'm wide awake, I'm going to go thank mom and dad, I'll call later" she said and hung up. I was happy that when I pitched the idea to my parents they were accepting, I know it was hard for them, but I knew I could manage and with the help of Sasha it will be easier. I just didn't want them to worry all the time and to get their life back.

I finished up eating and made my way to work, I went to my office to see Caitlyn already there and talking to a tall man. I made my way over and made eye contact with Caitlyn and she got scared and worried for a moment.

"Miss Black, this is just my friend Damon, he was bringing me to work" she said, and I didn't really care who it was when I walked in but now I certainly do.

"Pleasure to meet you Miss Black, I've heard nothing but good things" he said and held his hand out to me.

"Pleasure is all mine, though I've heard nothing about you" I said back, and the smirk came upon my lips as he stepped back and I looked to Caitlyn to see her conflicted with our interaction.

"I expect you in my office Miss Pierce" I said and turned around and went into my office.

"Of course" I heard her whisper as I shut the door behind myself. Who the hell was this guy, he seemed more than a friend with how close he was to her, and I have never seen him before so why now. Has she moved on from me? I shook my head, I shouldn't care if that even was the case, she can date whoever she likes. Why do I care so much?

I paced in front of the window looking out at the city down below as I heard a knock and the door opened, and I turned to see Caitlyn.

"Morning, this is about work right?" she asked as she kept her hands in front of her and began to shift her body weight from one leg to the other. I still hadn't said anything as she called for me again and I focused on her face.

"Yes, of course, what else would it be about?" I said and made my way to the desk, and she stayed quiet, speak to me please.

"I wasn't sure if it was because I brought Damon up without a pass?" she asked, as a matter of fact, I don't want him in the building ever again. My inner thoughts were screaming to come out, but I clenched my left fist, and she noticed this as I felt her come forward and place her hand over mine making me release the tension.

"Are you jealous Miss Black?" she asked, and I felt the heat rise in my cheeks and I quickly snatched my hand back and looked at her.

"What a preposterous thing to insinuate? Of course I'm not" I said, and I was trying to convince myself let alone her.

"Sure you aren't" she teased, and I stood up to gain the height on her, but I've learnt she doesn't fear that anymore.

"Why would I be jealous of a tall, dark, handsome man bringing you to work when very clearly you can make your own way. Why would I be jealous of that?" I said and instantly regretted all of that as I fell into her trap, and I closed my eyes shut fearing what she was going to say.

"You're right, why would you be jealous of that? I'll be at my desk if you need me" she said and left the office, and I punched the desk knowing she got the better of me and made me crack.

I felt a sickening feeling in my stomach, and I knew it was my anxiety coming back. Why am I getting so worked up over this one person? I have never been attracted to anyone since my college days and that was the last of it, I never expected to date again due to my work but then this woman comes into my life, and I can't shake her away.

She took the risk to try and get to know me, to want to know me and even took a greater risk and kissed me and I have allowed it, I haven't fired her or punished her for it. The realisation suddenly hits me, and I come to figure out that I like it, I like the attention, I like someone wanting to go that far for someone like me. But when she stopped and broke away, I lost all hope and felt more lonely than usual. So when she does talk to me I have to fight the urge to not smile or get lost in her eyes like I almost did just then.

Was I attracted to Caitlyn? Absolutely. Did I enjoy her presence? 100 percent. Was I falling for her? It was hard to say.

I remember that I still had to give her work as she was out there just waiting for me, so I grabbed a piece of paper I wrote on the tasks for today and left my office as she looked up from her desk.

"I need you to check on these projects today and make sure they are on task, while I have meetings with the heads of the projects" I tell her, and she nods and begins to get up as she grabs her tablet, but I grabbed her wrist as she turned to me and raised her eyebrow.

"Anything else Miss Black?" she asks, and I leaned in as I watch her eyes follow my movements.

"Will you have lunch with me?" I asked and I seemed to have caught her at a crossroads and she began to think of her answer.

"I don't think that's a good idea" she returned, but I knew I had to get her to agree, I had to start somewhere like she did.

"It'll be my treat, please" I begged, and my face softened to her, and she gave in and nodded as I let go of her wrist and she left to work as I went back into my office smiling like an idiot. I had to bring back my stony exterior for this meetings until lunch. I was counting down the hours.

These meetings were boring me to death. They must talk around the same thing about ten times before they truly understand the plan. But we finally got the plans finished and I was thankful the nightclub has been approved and will be finished in the next couple months.

As soon as it concluded I spoke with the heads that attended the meeting with me then I sprinted out of there back to my office, I grabbed what I needed, made myself more presentable and then left. I made my way to the ground floor and outside to see Caitlyn waiting for me with her arms crossed.

"Ten minutes over my lunch, I better get them back" she said and walked to where my car was, and I caught up with her.

"I apologise for keeping you waiting, you know how work is" I teased her, and she shook her head as I opened the passenger side door for her, and she gave me a quizzical look but got in as I closed the door and went to my side.

The drive was filled with music playing from the radio and I took her to the same sushi place she bought food at when I arrived. We walked in and got a table as we grabbed the menus and decided on what to eat.

"Good place to choose" she said, and I looked over my menu to see her already looking at me.

"Well this place actually has a special meaning" I told her, and she placed her menu down and leaned in to match me.

"Oh and what might that be?" she said as her teeth bit down on her lower lip and I let my eyes slip down but rose them back up.

"Well, it was our first lunch together, so it means that when I eat sushi, I think about you" I said and I saw the light tint come to her cheeks as she sat back and grabbed her menu, clearly taken aback by my abruptness. Was I trying too hard?

The waitress came and took our order, and we spent the time waiting with Caitlyn asking me how the meetings went, and which projects are close to getting finished. She was happy the nightclub was approved and still felt bad for the business trip, but I told her not to worry as I didn't want her to feel blame for that. I may never find out what happened or why it did, but I didn't need to know. Just making sure she was safe was the main priority in that situation.

When our food came the conversation continued as we joked a little about the dishes we had but we never spoke about our personal lives, I could see she was holding back but she did it well. I was quite proud that she was able to not make it about my life or say something to ruin this atmosphere, it was nice. But I was the one to ask a question this time.

"I have a question, and this doesn't make me jealous or anything, okay?" I told her and she squinted her eyes at me as she ate but she nodded to let me continue with my question, "That guy, Damon was it, why did he drive you to work?" I asked and the biggest smirk came on her face, I blushed and looked away from her.

"And you're asking this because you aren't jealous right?" she teased, and I looked her in the eyes.

"Just answer the question Caitlyn" I asked her, and she placed her fork down and started to think before answering me.

"First of all to set your mind at ease, we didn't sleep together" she told me, and I released a breath I didn't know I was holding in.

"So, who is he to you?" I asked and she took longer to think of an answer, she knew what to say but wanted to word it properly.

"We dated in university but when we broke up, we stayed friends. After I left work yesterday I called him since he knows about my past. We ended up at Caleb and Conor's, since Caleb had an appointment today, Damon drove me to work. That's the truth, I promise" she told me, I knew it was the truth, her voice broke mentioning her past and I'm beginning to think about what may have happened to her.

I didn't respond to her answer as I watched her, she was looking down and began fidgeting with her hands again and then found the tablecloth interesting as she began to pick at it. She looked up and caught me staring at her as she bit her lip waiting for a response.

"I understand but what exactly happened in your past?" I asked and I treaded carefully, she closed her eyes and bit her lip hard, I thought she was going to draw blood but thankfully she didn't.

"I can't tell you right now, but I will, just give me time, can you give me that?" she asked me, and I reached across the table, took her hand in mine and rubbed my thumb across the back of it.

"Of course, just know that I'm here if you ever need to talk" I told her, and she finally gave me a genuine smile and we were finally getting back on track.

We finished up lunch and then made our way back to work, on the drive though I noticed the glances she was taking at me and kept trying to talk but I didn't answer due to driving. I knew she couldn't keep it together so as I parked in my space I turned to her and caught her staring.

"See something you like?" I teased and arched my eyebrow at her, and she smirked back at me as she undid her seatbelt and turned to face me as I copied her actions and did the same.

"Very much yeah" she said, and I watched as her eyes travel up and down, not even bothering to hide checking me out.

I reached forward and grabbed her chin to look me in the eyes, "There will be time for that, right now I think we should get back to work" I said, and she blushed and pulled out my grasp.

The conversation ended as we got out the car. I didn't say anything else, I was enjoying the flirting and teasing. I think she was as well, if it makes us grow closer, it's worth it, I opened the door to the building for her and she gave me a big smile.

We took the elevator up and I made my way to the office allowing her to follow since I had documents to show her. She put her bag down and followed me into the office, a woman was standing at the window with her back to us but as she turned around all the air left my body, and I choked up.

A woman the same height as me, her long black hair cascaded down her back and over her shoulders. Wearing a sleek black backless dress with matching heels, her skin as ivory as mine but the crimson red lipstick she wore brought your attention there, her ocean blue eyes staring right at mine as the corners of her lips twisted into a sadistic smirk as she took steps towards me. The heels added inches to her height making her tower over me and I felt so small in this moment.

"I'm sorry can we help you?" Caitlyn asked her and the woman took a glance to her and laughed then focused back on me.

"River, you never introduced or told her about me" she said, that voice, I had forgotten how she sounded, and it pierced through my ears, but my voice was gone.

"Who are you?" Caitlyn asked again and she looked towards her and cracked a smile to her.

"Well pleasure to meet you darling, I'm Persephone Black, the rightful heir to this company."

Chapter Eight

PERSEPHONE

2009

The drive to the prison was agonising, I started to think back to what has happened over the last month in my head. I took the fall for my father's stupidity and now I would have to pay the price for seven years. For the organisation my father is working for, he was committing false accounting, money fraud, and he couldn't get out of it, not with how much he worked to get where he was. I never understood why he asked me to do it or why I agreed, his last words to me as I was cuffed and taken away were, 'in good time I will repay you.' My mother didn't understand and just couldn't look at me, thinking I betrayed the family and stole from them. My youngest sister Darcy wasn't even present so I couldn't say goodbye to her. But my younger sister, River, was in tears sobbing against my mom and trying to fight the guards to see me and give me one last hug. They granted her that and she didn't want me to go but I had to. I gave her a kiss on the head and promised to see her soon. That never happened.

As I arrived I had to go through all the checks as they made sure I smuggled nothing inside, I had to give up everything I had on me and then I was given an orange uniform to wear, was given the necessities and escorted to my new home for seven years. I was left alone for a moment as I sat on my bed, and it finally dawned on me, as I curled up and cried by myself. A month after I had been there, I was figuring out how things worked around the place, and I was moved to another part of the prison where I would get time to go outside and bunked with another woman. I had eyes on me all the time, I figured they knew what I did to get here but I overheard a conversation and they all thought I was attractive and that started to scare me.

I was only 20 years old, probably the youngest here and I had no one to rely on or help me through this, I had made no friends or enemies yet thankfully. But as an older woman started to approach me, I knew that was about to change. She eyed me up and down as I was sat on the ground against a wall.

"You're the new kid around here aren't you?" she asked, and she crouched down to get to eye level with me. I just nodded, too scared to speak up. She was around her late thirties; she had dark black short dreads and her olive skin shone under the sun. Her dark eyes burned into me as I noticed the slit through her eyebrow. She had tattoos all over her body and was very toned which I noticed on her arms as she wore a white tank top.

"What's your name and answer with your last name, that's how we address each other here?" she asked, and I cleared my throat and spoke to her.

"Black" my voice trembled, and she nodded and then stood up and held a hand out to me, I didn't do anything for a moment, and she didn't move so I took her hand, and she helped me up.

"I'm Remington but call me Remy" she said, and I nodded to her and held my arm in front of my body as I still didn't know what she wanted. "Come say hi to some friends of mine yeah?" she asked, and I shook my head, and she came closer, and I took a step back but was met with the wall. "Look kid, you got time here I can tell, you want to make friends sooner rather than later and I'm offering you a way here" she said, and I frowned at that, she must have been here longer than most people. I slowly nodded and she escorted me to her friends who welcomed me, and I tried remembering their names. There were ten other women so I would have to learn as the days went on.

3 months after being in prison, I was getting to learn the ropes as I found out that the girls I was hanging out with were sort of the 'popular' group and I noticed other people making requests to the girls I was with and then repaying them with food or items that they needed. I never did any requests yet, Remy just kept me at her side and told me to watch and learn from the other girls and that's exactly what I was doing. I was lucky that my bunkmate was one of the girls in this group, Miller she was a riot, always loud, but she had your back when needed. A week ago I was corned by three girls from another block and Miller came to my rescue and threatened them all which they didn't care about, but she got me out of there safely, so I trusted her from there on out.

After the requests were made they all returned just to take in the sun and talk a little. I undid the jumpsuit I wore and wrapped the sleeves around my waist as I wore a white t-shirt underneath and I laid back on my elbows to take in the sun. I caught one of the girls eyes, Reyes and she smirked at me as I rolled my eyes and looked away.

"You're a dainty pretty thing aren't you; you need some muscle on you girl" she said as she sat next to me and leaned back on one hand to get closer to me.

"I don't need muscle; my presence is enough to scare anyone" I told her which resulted in a laugh as I turned my head to look at her.

"Well, try harder, I'm not scared by you, to be honest, I think you're very pretty" she said and tried to get closer as Remy pushed her away from me resulting in her falling to the ground.

"Leave her alone Reyes, she doesn't want any of what you are offering" she said, and I turned to look at her as she smiled at me, "Take a walk with me kid" she said and got up to walk and I quickly followed her.

We walked to a bench away from most people as she sat down and I beside her, she was silent for a moment as we just stared out at the grounds.

"You've been with us for a few months now and I want to think I can trust you" she began, and I nodded to her and just remained silent. "Our group isn't any ordinary group, on the outside we are larger and more dangerous as being part of Don Bruno Orsini' Mafia in Italy" she told me, and I was speechless and didn't know how to react.

"Oh" was all I could say, and she took that to continue speaking.

"We have travelled to the US but it's not as notorious as our work in Italy, obviously we all got caught here" she said and gestured to herself and the other girls and now it finally clicked how they are so close with each other, "But since you don't have as high as a sentence as all of us, you are the one to leave and travel to Italy to continue the progress and make it there" she tells me and I shook my head, I didn't want this, I didn't want to live that sort of life.

"No, look I just want to do my time and get out, I never wanted this, I didn't agree to this" I said but she took my hand as I had stood and began to pace.

"Black look, you can do this, I'll teach you all I know in the time you have here, you got it" she said, and I shook my head, this is not me, I don't want that life.

"No, I'm sorry" I said and pulled my hand away and I walked away from something that could now put me in danger.

2010

The girls didn't mess with me or talk to me again since I said I didn't want to be part of their group, for ten months things were okay. I wasn't messed with, I felt like it would get easier to make it through this. I spent my 21st birthday alone and I realised that my family was never going to come see me and I think that was for the best.

I was enjoying my time alone in the courtyard as I was reading a book to pass the time when a couple of girls came over to harass me. They thought I was part of Remy's group still but as much as I tried to say no, they wouldn't accept it. One girl threatened me with a razor she made, and another held me by the throat. I looked around frantically trying to find a guard but to no avail, so I took matters into my own hands. The girl who was choking me, I slapped her across the face making her release me and as she bent down, I let my foot connect with her face as the other girl charged for me and I dodged and pushed her up against the chain-link fence and kicked her across the stomach. The other girl did get a slice on me and that's when Remy and her girls saw what was happening and rushed over to help and disarm the girl as I held my side trying to stop the blood flow.

"Let's take her to medical quick" Martinez said as she held me as Remy quickly came to my other side and they helped me.

I was laying on the bed in the infirmary with a bandage around my abdomen to stop the bleeding and I know it'd leave a nasty scar. The girls and myself were the only ones in the room as the girls who attacked me were sent to isolation for who knows how long.

"You held yourself pretty well until a weapon got involved" Remy said as she stood at the end of the bed, and I sat up and shrugged.

"I took self-defence classes at 15, nothing special" I got of the bed and the girls were surprised I was okay to continue like nothing happened.

"Look, I know you don't want to join us, but there is fight clubs and that can earn you respect and protection from other people, you know we have your back" Remy tells me, and I listen to her words. I made my way to the door but turned back to them.

"I'll check it out but doesn't mean I'll join" I said and left the infirmary to go back to my cell.

Over the next few weeks, I went to see these fight clubs to see how they worked and what the competition seemed like. I was intrigued and it would help to pass the time and get some rage out of my system so when the next one came up I signed up and waited to see who I'd be up against. And much to my surprise it was the girl who tried to shank me. Reyes made her way over to me once the girls noticed I came, "Hey, if you win this, I'll give you a reward" she said as she eyed my body and gave me a wink.

"You're not my type" I said as I didn't even look at her and she feigned hurt as she held her chest.

"So what is your type, Martinez? Jackson? Or is Remy more your type? You like being dominated?" she asked, naming a few of the girls as I turned to her as my name was called.

"In the end, everyone will submit to me" I said and patted her cheek leaving her speechless as I went to the ring they made as the girl who I was against laughed that I was her opponent.

"This'll be easy, how's the injury sweetheart?" she mocked me, and I continued to ignore her and looking at her and seeing anything I can use to my advantage to wipe the smug smile from her face.

As the bell rung, I watched her run for me, and I side stepped her seeing her best strategy is all offence. She went from punching to kicking and I watched how she does it and one time I grabbed her leg to twist it making her fall and I stomped on the back of her knee making her cry out in pain. Then I sat on her back and went ahead to choke her out making her tap out quickly. I dropped her and got off as they raised my hand and I looked to the girls especially Remy and she just smiled and clapped for me. I smiled back and walked out the ring.

Things were about to change around here, and I was the pinnacle of that happening. Over the next couple of months, fight club became a weekly activity for the girls here. I was in various fights and I either left with bruises or broken bones, but I never lost. We were caught by a few guards and spent time in isolation to cool off, but I finally got on one of the guards good side and she let us do our thing in the basement. So most would sneak off to the basement for the fights.

Over time I was talking with Remy again and I joined the girls back because they started to recognise me as a threat through the fighting, I wasn't offended, it was the plan all along.

2011/2012

Over the next two years we had new inmates coming in and our group was still just the twelve of us, but I was seeking out new recruits to join us so when they get out I have contacts. I needed friends since family was no longer an issue for me. Even after three years they still didn't want to see me, even River. I thought she would be the one to always come but I guess I was wrong about her. I was snapped out of my thoughts as Remy snapped her fingers in front of me and I turned to look at her with the same resting bitch face I have donned since day one. "What?" I simply asked and she raised her hand from how blunt I am.

"Just wondering what you're thinking off?" she asked, and I turned my attention to the newbies doing what I used to do and stay to themselves.

"Looking for some new friends I guess" I said and pointed to who I was eyeing and sent three of the girls to go recruit the three inmates I was watching.

I had become Remy's second in command because she was leaving in a year, and I had to learn all what I needed. I had no idea why she was getting released early but I didn't question it. I still have years on my sentence so I would become leader when she left. I started making a name for myself, all the inmates knew me and feared me, and the guards would just let things slide. I didn't want special treatment, but I wasn't complaining. I headed to my cell which had gotten bigger over the years, and I was closer to the girls as well. I grabbed the notebook I kept and started writing down memories from today. I started to journal every day to keep a memoir of my time here. It isn't the best time but it's something I will think back on in time.

I was interrupted by the guard who allowed us the privacy of the basement for the fights.

"Black?" she called out to me, and I closed the journal and turned to look at her.

"What do you want?" I asked her and she slipped into the cell, and I stood up and moved away to keep my distance.

"I can't keep allowing the fights, the other guards are questioning why most of the inmates have bruises and broken bones, it has to stop" she said, and I raised an eyebrow and stepped closer to her.

"Well try and assure them that it's what inmates do, they fight because they feel like caged animals, can you do that for me sweetheart?" I said and raised my hand up to grab her chin to make her look at me and I saw the look in her eye. She was scared but also turned on. She nodded and I gripped harder, I hated when people didn't answer me with words. I'm not a mind reader.

"Yes ma'am" she said, and I smirked and released her as she left. I peered out the cell and looked up to the second level to a cell as I saw the same woman who had been eyeing me for everyday for the last month. She was watching me again, I decided to see what her deal was and blew her a kiss and went back in my cell, I needed to find out who she was.

2012 was here rather fast and it was the day Remy had to leave, we threw a little going away party for her and in time I'd gotten to know her, I know she'll be a good ally and contact to have on the outside world. We said our goodbyes as only three of us were allowed to watch her leave the prison and I thought back to our talk the night before.

"Some people will try and fight you and try to be better, don't let them, make sure they know their place even if it makes you hated" she told me, I wrote it in my journal, and she reached out a hand to stop me writing. "You know all this; you don't need to write it down" she said, and I looked at her for a long time before I slowed closed the book and placed it down.

We spent the entire night talking and reminiscing and now she has gone to probably live life the same way as before. Me and the girls that came with headed back to the cells and were stopped by a rival gang we had become familiar with over the last couple of months.

"Seems your leader has finally been released, you girls need someone in charge, and I offer my services only you will be our errands girls and lap dogs more than anything" Richards said and laughed with the others, I ushered my girls forward and I shoulder checked Richards on my way out and she grabbed my arm to stop me. As I turned I grabbed her arm and twisted it around her back and slammed her into the wall. Before her girls grabbed me, my two were already there holding them back.

I kicked Richards in the back of her knees to make her kneel before me, I released her arm and instead grabbed her roughly by the chin and used my other hand to pull her hair back to look me in the eye.

"You better listen because I'm not going to repeat myself" I started off and she nodded quickly, and I could see her eyes were wide as I put fear into her life. "You stay away from my girls and me, if I see you or your people bullying or scaring other inmates, I will personally end you, got it?" I whispered in her ear, and she nodded quickly to answer, and I pulled her head back and then slammed it against the wall making her wince and cry out, but I covered her mouth with my hand that was holding her chin to keep her quiet. "Use your words Richards" I spoke to her, and she mumbled against my hand, so I moved it to hear her.

"Understood" she said, and I released her and looked to my girls as they released them, and they followed me.

I walked into my cell to see the girl who has been watching me for a while sitting on my bed. I peered out the cell to make sure I wasn't seeing things and looked back, and she was indeed sitting there. "Are you lost or something?" I asked and she smiled and stood up.

"No, just seeing what I was dealing with" she said and was about to leave but I blocked her exit and crossed my arms.

"You've been watching me for months, who the hell are you? Do you know me or something?" I asked and she took a step back.

"Not yet but I hope I will" she said, and she was being quiet about why she is here, and I didn't blame her, I've seen girls over the years do the same tactic and it always ends the same way.

"Just tell me if you know me or not, I hate these silly games" I asked her, and she sat down again, and I walked more into the cell.

"I know your family, but you are a blur, on the outside it's hardly like you exist, yes it's said that the Black family has three daughters, but only River and Darcy are mentioned. It's like you are dead or something" she said and just hearing my sisters names was enough for me to reach out and grabbed her by the throat and pin her down onto the bed and I held her in that position, and she grabbed my arm to try and release tension, but I didn't let up.

"Say my sisters names one more time, I fucking dare you!" I shouted and I caught the attention of other inmates who could see what was unfolding. She tried to catch her breath, but she was losing the battle here, but she got to live as Martinez rushed in and pulled me off her.

"Black calm down, don't kill her" she was holding me, but she lost her grip as I launched myself at the woman and punched her in the face causing her to be knocked back against the bed as blood starting to drip from her nose.

Martinez got hold of me again with the help of Reyes and Jones as the woman got up holding her nose. She gave me a look of fear and mercy and she ran out the cell. Once the girls figured I was calm they let me go and I shrugged them off.

"You three watch her, anything seems suspicious, you tell me" I told them, and they gave each other a look but nodded to me and left the cell.

I hit the wall a few times and knew something wasn't right with that conversation, she knew my family and that wasn't good. I decided to take a shot in the dark and went to the phonelines and tried to reach out and made a call.

It rang and rang for what seemed an eternity and eventually it went through, and no voice was heard, and I knew I'd break at hearing her voice.

"Persephone?" I heard and I heard the tremble in River's voice, and I had to hold it together.

"River" I said, and we both broke down in tears just hearing each other's voices.

"I don't have long just listen to me, watch out for the family especially Darcy, she is your responsibility, don't let anything happen to her, you hear me?" I told her and she tried to ask why but I didn't say anything else.

"You have to uphold the name, I love you" I said and hung up the phone. I steadied my breathes and ran a hand through my hair. Why is everything so fucked? I walked away and just went outside to get air and clear my head.

2013

A new year came, and I was awakened one day with a guard shaking me awake and in that instance I lashed out and I was lucky it was the nice guard who let us get away with everything.

"Easy Black, you got a visitor" she said, and I raised my eyebrow, I never have visitors, I took every one of my list.

"Impossible" I said and turned back over in my bunk.

"Well you do, don't leave him waiting" she said and left my cell, and I was intrigued that this might be a joke, but I had to go to see who this 'him' was.

I made myself more presentable and went to the visitors sector and I looked around the room to see no one I knew as the guard pointed to a middle-aged man who was here to see me. I had no idea who he was. He was around his fifties, grey hair combed into a neat style with a bushy beard that rounded his face more. He had dark brown eyes that were almost black, and he wore a grey suit and seemed prestigious, but I couldn't still guess who he was. I sat down opposite him and eyed him more closely.

"Who are you?" I asked and he smiled and laughed, and I heard the deep hoarse voice he had.

"Pleasure to make your acquaintance, I'm Bruno Orsini" he said, and I instantly heard the Italian accent and my eyes widened as I knew that name. It was the same name that Remy told me about, the mafia leader and I sat up straighter and held out my hand which he was shocked by but took it. "May I know your real name, not what they call you here?" he asked, and I was in shock with this whole arrangement. Was this Remy's doing?

"Persephone Black" I said, and he nodded and smiled at me.

"I mean no harm, your friend Remy had me come see you, said you are special, and I wanted to see what all the fuss was about" he said, and my suspicions were right, and I crossed my arms.

"Can you cut to the chase Don Orsini" I said, and he smiled liking that I called him Don, knowing that I was already agreeing to join his cause.

"I can get you out in a years' time, when you do, you go to this location" he passed me a slip of paper which I quickly hid on me, "There will be money, a passport and a ticket. You use that to come to Italy and you join us as a family" he said, and I nodded to him.

"Thank you" I said, and he nodded, we were told time was up, we both stood, and I saw other people quickly hug their relatives and I yearned for that, the Don shook my hand again and brought me closer.

"You'll be out soon, I assure you" he said, and I nodded and pulled away.

"Is Remy okay?" I asked wanting to know if she is safe and looked after.

"She is" he said and then left as I headed back to my cell. I only have a year, till I'm out and I was happy to not serve the full sentence.

2014

The day I was to leave I couldn't have been happier, the years I spent that weren't even mine to serve were finally over and I knew I had a place to go to afterwards. I said goodbye to my girls and told them that I would help get them all out as soon as possible and we'd be reunited again. I did my last checks and got changed back into the clothes I arrived in, knowing that they were outdated, and I had to get new ones soon. I left the prison with what I came with and found myself lost already. I took out the piece of paper the Don gave me and began walking to where the location was.

It was a safety deposit locker storage and I input the code to the locker that was written down and opened it to see what the Don said was in there. Money, a passport, a plane ticket and a cell phone. I unlocked the phone and went to contacts to see the Dons number and Remy's. I called her first knowing that she'd be happy to hear my voice and vice versa.

"Black?" she answered as soon as the call went through.

"The one and only, I'm heading to the airport right now, see you in 13 hours" I told her, and I called out for a cab and got in.

"See you soon Black, it's been too long" she said, and we hung up and I was happy to start a new life.

The flight was painful but as soon as we touched down, I made a beeline to the departure pickups since I had no luggage and as soon as I saw Remy, I ran as fast as I could and jumped into her arms as she caught me and spun me around.

"Gosh, it's so good to see you" she said, and she placed me down, but we kept hugging, and I couldn't believe she is here right now, we both are out and free.

"I've missed you so much" I told her and held her tighter.

"There will be time to catch up, let's get you some food and a change of clothes" she said and pulled back and held my face in her hands to look at me and I was crying and smiling so wide.

"Come, let's go" she said and wrapped her arm around me as we left the airport, and she took me to get some food which was divine and to get me a change of clothes to look more like I wasn't 20 years old anymore.

Then we got in her car and had a quick drive to a private estate where a large mansion stood strong on a hill surrounded by greenery, shrubs and hedges all around and flowerbeds along the front lawn. Three expensive cars were sitting out front and off to the side were five black SUVs, this was a dream home. We pulled up, got out and stood side by side as I gawked at this large masterpiece of a building.

"Welcome home" Remy said, and we entered my new home.

Chapter Nine

PERSEPHONE

2014

We walked into the warm home; it was like walking into a showroom. Everything was spotless, the house was covered in mahogany from the staircase to the flooring as well as the trimmings around the windows. The main foyer was as large as half a basketball court, an overlook from an interior balcony that just showed the size of the three-story mansion and different rooms leading off from this one.

Remy placed her hand on my shoulder and took me to one of the rooms, where there was a large wall full of books and a poker table with eight chairs surrounding it. We walked through that room to an outside patio where the Don sat reading a paper with a lit cigar in his mouth.

"Don Orsini, I bring Miss Black" Remy said, pushing me forward as the Don got up. He brought me into his arms for a hug and then had me sit down as Remy also joined us.

"How was your flight?" he asked me, folding up the newspaper and taking the cigar out of his mouth.

"Long" I said, and he smiled at my short reply.

"I'm sure you know enough from Remy so I'm not going to tell you again but you are free to live here as long as the rules that are set are followed and you don't fuck up, capiche?" he asked and I nodded and then verbally replied knowing how much I myself dislike responses like this.

"Yes sir" I said, and he smiled and gave me a credit card so I could buy a new wardrobe for myself.

My room was on the top floor and the last one that was free, there wasn't much, just a bed, empty walk-in closet, a few dressers and I had an ensuite off to the side. So I spent the day with Remy as I got myself a whole new wardrobe, furniture for my room and all the necessities I would need. I even got a new phone since the one the Don had given me was a burner phone.

We got back home and joined the Don and the other members for dinner where they officially had me join the family and I was given a signet ring as proof. The ring was quite large and made of silver, the emblem on it was of a phoenix with small gems encrusted into it, I wore it with a smile on my face finally feeling like I belonged somewhere.

Over the next couple of months of living in Italy, I learned the Italian language so I could make my way around more easily. There would be times where I would be taught by Remy but as I walked the streets, listening to the people speak, I could pick up what they were on about with the words I recognised. It was a learning experience all the time.

Throughout the months I was taught about the different Mafia families that lived in Italy, the one we had to watch out for though was the family of Hector Esposito. They deal in the drug business and do their business in pool halls as they own ten of them. I was told as my first assignment to infiltrate one of the pool halls and find out as much as possible. I agreed to it and that leads us to tonight.

I got dressed to look as if I was going out to have a good time. I wore a solid black cut out halter neck dress that was tight and hugged my curves perfectly. I wore a decent amount of light make up and had my hair straight down my back. I grabbed my clutch and got one of the chauffeurs to take me to where I needed to go.

It was a very elegant pool hall, I had to give ID at the entrance and as I entered it was lit nicely, not too bright or too dark, the colours were modest of blacks and greys. I made my way to the bar, ordered a cocktail and took a seat just to get my bearings. I made a call to Remy to play the part of being stood up.

"Hey I just made it, what time are you getting here?" I said and looked around to see if I caught anyone's attention yet.

"Oh darling you are so sexy when you call, I'm tempted to come" Remy teased me, and I just rolled my eyes at her playfulness, I wished I could say something else back, but I had to stick to this role.

"But you said you would take me out tonight, this keeps happening" I said and tried my best to seem upset and pissed off while Remy was howling with laughter on the other side. As I scanned the room, I locked eyes with a brunette who was watching me from a side door which I assumed was private for the rival gang, so I gave a little smile and turned around to add mystery to the situation.

"I know, I'm such a dick, look you have fun but not too much fun, I'll come get you in three hours okay babe" she said, and I couldn't answer in my usual manner to her childish self, but I stuck to my script.

"You know what just forget it, don't call me again" I said, hung up and slammed my phone down as I downed my cocktail. I was about to ask for another, but the brunette had made her way over and got the attention of the bartender first.

"Prendo un Boulevardier e un altro di quello che sta bevendo questa signora, grazie" she said and I smiled at the way her voice sounded, strict yet sweet, as she took a seat next to me and looked at me, her dark grey eyes caught my attention along with her sharp jawline and full eyebrows. She smiled at me showing her perfect white teeth, the smell of mint intoxicating me, and I was suddenly very interested in her.

"Italiano o inglese?" she asked, and I knew what those words meant so I responded.

"Inglese" I said, and she smiled at me and thanked the bartender for our drinks as we clinked them and took a small sip.

"You're a bit overdressed for a pool hall aren't you?" she asked, I was shocked to hear her perfect English, the accent was still there but she spoke better than most people I know.

"I was supposed to be having a date, but I got stood up" I said and sipped my drink again, trying my best to not get distracted but it was a lost battle from the get-go.

"How can a man stand up such a beautiful lady?" she said, shamelessly checking me out smirking as she did.

"I never said it was a man" I said and raised my eyebrows at her, making her smile.

"So let me entertain you tonight, how about a few games of pool, then I take you out on the streets and show you what Italy is made of?" she offered and that was my ticket in and I had to accept but at this point I think I was going to accept for an entirely different reason.

"Okay yeah, let's do it…" I trailed and let myself linger hoping she would drop her name.

She downed the rest of her drink, got up and held out her hand to me, "I'm Luiza."

"Persephone" I said and took her hand as she led me to a table for our first game.

It was awkward at first as we started playing but soon we got into it, and I got to show my skills. She even offered to show me techniques as she went behind me and leaned in close as her hand held onto mine and the other on my waist. I closed my eyes feeling her close to me and inhaled her perfume, the scent of lavender becoming a favourite of mine. We had drinks and got to know each other which was nice to not speak of work or anything to do with the mafia but that feeling was in the back of my mind.

She took me on a small tour of the area we were in. Showing where the best restaurants were, activities I could do when I had free time and I learnt that she was indeed born here by the way she was enthusiastically talking about her home. I was hooked on every word she said, and I forgot why I was even here in the first place.

Work never crossed the conversation, but I got to know her as a person instead and she was very charming and interesting, I wanted to talk to her all night but sadly all good things have to come to an end as Remy texted to see where I was and I redirected her to come get me. Luiza waited with me, and I spotted Remy's car and pointed it out.

"There's my ride, thank you for a lovely time, I hope we can do this again sometime soon" I said as I held my phone in my hand signalling that I wanted her number which she gave me.

She took my hand and planted a kiss on top and smiled at me "Text me when you are home safe" she said, I smiled and felt warm inside, very unusual for me to feel that.

"I will, goodnight Luiza" I said as she released my hand, and I began to walk to the car.

"Buonanotte Persephone" she said and went her own way as I got in the car, and we drove away.

Remy and I spoke a little on the way home, but I only told her a few details since I didn't really get anything as I was more on a date then doing the actual job, but as we walked inside, the Don was already there waiting and motioned me to follow him. We got to the poker room and as we sat down, he lit up another cigar.

"So, how did it go, did you learn anything?" he asked, and I had to say something to prove I was capable, so I told him what I did know and maybe just made some stuff up.

"They use the pool halls as their main source of product moving, there was a private door that was being used a lot and they have people always around watching everyone's move. They had suppliers in and out for the time I was there so something had been delivered, but I couldn't tell what" I said and hopefully he didn't see through my lie.

"Well done, you did good for your first assignment, go up and rest" he said and seemed to believe me, I nodded and went to my room as fast as I could, panicking from being found out as a liar.

2015

The next few months I was sent on more assignments to different pool halls and those times without a distraction I was able to find out way more than the first time. They are definitely distributing drugs from the halls. I got licence plate numbers from the vehicles used and got them all back to the Don without being followed once. I was climbing the ranks in the mafia and wondered how far I'd go, I mentioned to the Don about the girls in prison, he said he'd deal with it but never brought it up again. I promised the girls help and I didn't want to let them down. They took me in when I was at my lowest when I first arrived at the prison, they didn't have to, but they did. I felt like I owe it to them, and I did tell them that I would find a way to get them out, already a couple years have passed, and I haven't even got one of them released yet so hopefully I can start on that soon.

I got information on my family back in the states and found out my family was doing amazingly with their own corporation, and I felt angry as I was basically forgotten about, but I'd get payback when I met with father one day.

Remy and I were called to the Don one day and were told that one of his people had been taken and was being held as a hostage, so we were to go get them back. Her name is Janet she is a former army solider, great when it came to infiltration and getting information out of people, so she is a high value target, so no mishaps were to happen.

We headed out and began the long drive to an abandoned warehouse that was four stories high, as we got out I sized up the place as Remy opened the trunk and let me choose what I wanted. I looked at the place again then back to the weapons and decided on taking a pocket knife and a Beretta 80 series. As I held the gun my hand started shaking as I had never taken another life. Remy soon placed her hand over mine.

"You don't have to do this, you can just stay behind and I'll go in" she offered but I shook my head and steeled myself.

"No, it's okay, I got this" I said and grabbed extra clips as I saw Remy take a Benelli M1014 and a belt of knives before we headed inside the warehouse.

I had practised shooting over the last few months knowing that at some point I would have to learn, and it still felt unreal to take a life, but Remy didn't seem to care as she must have done it before. As we headed in we took cover and focused on the walk patterns of the people, there were two up above looking down and three on the same floor as us.

As one came close to Remy, she kicked him and took him as a meat shield as the two above focused on her. I stayed in cover and focused my aim, shot two men quickly and the gunfire drew the other two guys closer to us but with two quick shots, I took another out as did Remy. She questioned her meat shield to where they held the hostage and hearing him tell her the top floor, she shot the guy in the leg and then we made our way up the next floors.

I tried not to think too much about the lives I was taking and just kept moving forward, I could worry about it after. We killed the people in our way, I stayed mostly in cover to make exact shots as Remy was just blasting with the shotgun and anyone that seemed too far away, she'd take a knife and throw it at them making bodies drop one after another. We got to the top floor where one room remained, we walked in to see a woman tied to a chair and it seemed to be our target.

"Took you long enough" she said as I went behind her and cut her free. Remy helped her up and to the door as I was quickly checking for anything I could use.

"Black, we got to go now!" Remy said but I told her to go, as I'd catch up, she didn't like that but had no choice as I continued to search around and found a ledger which would be useful. I grabbed it and was about to leave when someone rounded the door and smacked me in the face with something metal.

I hit the floor and regained my vision to see a large man with a crowbar. I grabbed my gun, but he kicked it out my grip and hit me in the side with the crowbar multiple times and I was to hurt to move so I just stayed where I was and luckily I wasn't unconscious.

He picked up my body and started to carry me outside as I slowly opened my eyes, I noticed he was taking me another way then where Remy was. I took a quick chance and shouted out her name and struggled out of his arms making me land on the ground as he kicked me hard in the stomach making me lose my breath. He tried to grab me again, as I stabbed my knife into his foot and his cry of pain was cut off as the loud sound of a shotgun made him stop and when I looked at him, I saw the blood start to stain his shirt as I scrambled away as he fell. Remy got to me quickly, lifted me up and took me back to the car to quickly drive away.

We got back without any more issues and as the three of us stumbled inside the Don looked us over. Giving Remy and me a nod then walking away with the woman we saved. I looked to Remy, as she helped me upstairs to my room, I needed to bathe or shower to then rest my body, I was hurt so much.

I stood in front of the mirror and unbuttoned my shirt leaving me in my bra as I looked at my body and winced as I ran my fingers over the now forming bruises all over my ribs and my stomach and I felt like crying. I opened my bag to the ledger I grabbed, and this might come in handy but it's all in Italian, I could only make out a few words, but it just seemed to be payments to different benefactors. Remy returned, closed my bedroom door and I saw her holding a bucket and cloth.

"Sit" she said, I looked to her and did as she asked as I sat on the edge of the bed, and she kneeled down in front of me. I saw the bucket of water and ice and knew this was going to suck. "Next time I say to leave, we leave, got it?" she said as she wet the cloth, rinsed it and started to dab the bruises, I was flinching at every touch.

"Yeah, I still got what I wanted though" I said as I pointed to the bag and then pulled away from her touch, "Ow, that fucking hurts!" I called out, she rolled her eyes and laughed at me.

"It's going to, just hold still" she said and tried again but I backed away moving back on the bed, but she wasn't going to stop. She climbed up on the bed and straddled my waist making the pain more unbearable as I gritted my teeth and groaned, I tried to push her off, but she dropped the cloth to her side and pinned my wrists down, I hated being overpowered. "Let me take care of you" she whispered as the tension was rising in the room.

I didn't say anything as I was focusing on the position we were in. Truthfully I did find Remy a very attractive woman, but I never felt anything more than just friendship between us. I just nodded when she spoke to me and surprisingly she released my wrists, grabbed the cloth again and began to dab the bruises. I didn't mind that she was still on me, I weirdly found it comforting that she wanted to stay with me and help me. After she did what she could, I showered and then walked out to see her still in my room, I laid down wincing, she sat next to me, not leaving me just yet.

"In time, it'll heal just never do that again" she said, and I hummed to her in response, but something still annoyed me.

"The Don didn't even care that I was hurt, what the fuck was that!" I said and Remy turned to me, seeing I was clearly not okay with the way he was.

"It's just how he is" she said, and I shook my head.

"It shouldn't be, a leader is to lead and look after what he calls 'a family', if I was in charge, I would change things around here" I said, and Remy just looked at me and laughed.

"Well you aren't so calm down and try to sleep" she said, kissed my head and went to the door, she gave me one more look and then left. I didn't sleep at all.

2017

The years went by in a flash but throughout that time I was getting closer to the Don and learned more than what I should have known, I think I even knew more than Remy, but I was taking it all in. I took moments in my free time to meet with Luiza on occasion. We got to know each other more and we had our first date, had more after that and agreed to continue dating. We haven't spoken in months though as we got caught once and when we learned that we were both members of rival gangs, we just agreed to keep our distance until something could be settled. But nothing ever came of that.

One day I was about to leave to meet with one of our suppliers for a new deal but heard shouting coming from the foyer. I ran to the railing and looked down to see our people as someone familiar was in the centre on their knees. I quickly ran down as I heard a slap echo through the home. I got to the bottom of the stairs as my eyes connected with Luiza and I stopped in my tracks.

"I found this spy, hiding in our hedges. She's from the Esposito family, I say we abuse and then kill her" he called out making everyone around him cheer. All the men agreed I looked to the woman who I knew, and they remained silent. I looked to Remy who seemed disgusted in what he said. I had to make a bold move now.

"No!" I called out making the cheers stop and he looked to me.

"You don't make choices around here, just because she's a woman, she's still a rival, she'll go back and tell them everything" he said, and the men remained agreeing with him.

"I'm not with the family anymore" Luiza called out, but he slapped her again and was about to give her another, but I stood in front of Luiza and grabbed his wrist.

"Swing for her again, I fucking dare you!" I shouted at him as I dug my nails into his wrist making him wince as I drew blood as he pulled himself free he glared at me, he was seething at this point.

Before anything else happened the Don's voice echoed through the place as the man in front of me moved away as the Don approached.

"Move!" he told me, and I knew what he was going to do so I remained where I stood, and Remy gave me a look to just move but I didn't.

"I can't" I whisper so only the Don could hear but I knew everyone was listening.

He leaned his head closer to me, "And why is that?" he questioned, I raised my head and blinked away the tears as I bit my lip.

"Because" I choked back my tears, "Because I love her" I said, and the silence was deafening but I heard the gasp come from Luiza.

"Move!" he shouted at me and even forcefully pushed me away as I stumbled I closed my eyes as I heard another slap and then the thud to see that it was a hard slap to make her hit the ground. He went behind her, picked her up by her hair and I was about to go forward, but I was stopped as two of the men held me back.

He kneeled down to be in the same position as Luiza and held a knife to her throat as he pulled her hair tight, and I saw the fear in her eyes.

"Let her go and give her a gun" the Don said as the men moved away and pressed a gun into my hand, but I kept my eyes on Luiza.

"Kill her to prove you are one of us, if you don't I slice her throat for you to just watch" I wasn't listening to anything he said, my eyes were on hers and she was terrified, but she kept her calm and managed to speak out.

"It's okay baby, just do it" she said and closed her eyes.

I was crying at this point as I lifted to gun to aim it, I released the safety as my hand trembled and I used the other to steady it.

"I'm sorry" was all I said as I shifted the sight and shot the Don right between the eyes. The sound was deafening, and I rushed forward quickly to remove the knife from anywhere near her, it only sliced into her a little. I quickly took off my shirt, held it against her neck as she lay against my chest as the Don lay in front of us drowning in his own blood.

"I got you, it's okay, sorry if that was loud" I said and before she could speak I kissed her, I didn't care who was watching right now. Everyone was shocked and didn't move a muscle. "Someone get me a first aid kit now!" I shouted and waited to see if anyone responded. I felt a presence next to me and I saw Remy so I gently laid Luiza down to let Remy treat the wound on her neck. I stood up as Janet handed me a new shirt to wear as she kneeled by Remy to help.

"Things are going to change from now on, I'm in charge and if anyone has a problem with that, you are free to leave but if you cross me, I'll end you myself" I said and waited. All the men left, the ones who had been here for years just walked out, all that remained were all the women. All looking to Luiza with sympathy and praising me for not letting it continue and taking a stand. I looked to all the woman and nodded, "Okay then, let's make a name for ourselves" I said, and they all agreed as the first rule of order was to remove the Don's body and clean the blood from the floor.

While that happened I took Luiza to my room to rest and as she was resting I went around the entire mansion and mapped out everything, even rooms I didn't even know about and memorised everything and planned what to do next. In the Don's room I found the key to his office but checked on Luiza before getting to business.

I walked into my room to see Luiza awake and looking around curiously, she caught my eye and smiled at me. "I thought all this was a dream and I just came to take you out for lunch" she made a joke out of the situation, and I smiled and sat by her and took her hand.

"I'm so glad you are okay" I said and used my free hand to caress her cheek where she was slapped.

"You saved my life" she said, and I nodded, she smiled and held my hand that was on her cheek.

"Did I also hear that you *love me*?" she asked, and I looked away as I felt the heat rise into my cheeks and making it noticeable on my pale skin.

"It was a moment of realisation, but I do yeah" I said and looked back at her eyes as she smiled softly at me.

"Ti amo Persephone" she said, and I exactly knew what that meant as I leaned forward, and our lips meet in a short but sweet kiss. I pulled away and kissed her again as we broke out into smiles.

"So, it seems weird asking this now but I'm still going to do it, will you be my girlfriend?" I asked her, she laughed and then held her neck the strain was not good for her.

"I think it's very clear, but to answer, I would love to be your girlfriend" she said and brought me into another kiss.

"I have some things to check on in the office to find out what all this was, are you okay to rest here?" I asked her but she was already getting up making me confused.

"I got sliced, my legs still work and right now, I don't want to be more than five feet from you" she said, and I had to agree with her there, I laced our fingers together to lead her to where the office was and unlocked it with the key I had found.

It was like any normal modern office. As I sat at the desk to look up things on the computer, Luiza started to go through files that were stacked on the shelves. I went through his computer once I found the password written down, he had collected information on my family all this time. My family was well known on the west side of the country, and I found a conversation between the Don and my father where there was a contract signed over to me for a company that I never even knew off. At least father stuck to his promise for that.

I continued searching and found all the Don's businesses and more illegal doings, but I was planning to stop all the illegal doings and focus on legit work instead to build up from that. I decided I would have to sign all the Don's possessions to my name that being banks, homes, everything he had. I spent time on scheduling meetings, and adding it all up, I was going to be a billionaire. I looked over to Luiza who found the signed contract between the Don and my father to see that it was real, and my name signed on it.

"Well, this is going to cause some chaos in the future when I return home" I said and smirked to myself, and Luiza looked at me and raised her eyebrow.

"You're sadistic under all that sexiness, aren't you" she said as she tried to kiss my cheek, but I wrapped my arms around her waist, pulled her onto my lap and into a kiss and then spoke against her mouth.

"Oh sweetheart, you have no idea" I said and kissed her again.

2018-24

The next couple of years were spent working every second of every day. I started with extending the mansion for more of the girls to live there. Meaning that for the girls that were still in prison I found loop holes in their cases to get them all released one after another and got them all to come to Italy so we could be together. The illegal businesses the Don had, were all ended, and I cut ties with all other gangs and even ended the rivalry with Luiza's former family.

I extended my Italian vocabulary with the help of Luiza and then took classes to learn German, Spanish and French. We extended the business, and I took a page out of my father's book to build a corporation for helping the people. We built homes for the homeless, we built and renovated orphanages in Italy and moved the business to the states as well, planning on making it worldwide. We gave food to shelters, helped people who were less fortunate and just did good in the world.

Luiza and myself got married in 2020 and decided to leave all this for Remy to continue since she was the one who helped me get started and took a chance on me when she really could have chosen anyone. I was just in the right place at the right time. So we left and rebuilt our own life back in California. I was in a different city to stay clear of my family for a while and eventually moved closer but didn't let them know at all. I never asked about the contract, about the company, but I always kept it on me for the right time to present itself.

Getting to my thirties, I knew one day I wanted to settle down with Luiza and start a family together. Once I was back in the states, I got a call from a woman who had been in prison with me, the same girl who knew my family the same one I almost choked to death. She had been watching my family for years and in 2023, she kidnapped Darcy, I couldn't do anything about it since my family didn't know I was near, and it might have seemed strange for me to come out of nowhere to help. But luckily I discovered that River had kept her promise and protected Darcy like I asked.

I was proud of River for how far she had come in life and what she had achieved but she needed to know the truth about everything. About me being imprisoned in our father's stead and to also know that what she has worked so hard for, is all for nothing since it's not even her name on the contract. I was standing in the kitchen holding a mug of coffee as I felt Luiza wrap her arms around me from behind.

"What are you thinking about amore mia?" she asked, and I turned in her arms as I placed the mug down and wrapped my arms around her shoulders.

"I think I'm going to go to the company and pay my sister a long awaited visit" I said and she nodded and gave me a quick kiss on my lips.

"If you think it's for the best, I'll support you" she said, and I could not ask for a better wife in all my life.

"I love you" I told her. I grabbed her chin, gave her a long kiss and then bit her bottom lip to tease her.

"Don't start with that now, go to the company" she said and tried to escape my grasp, but I pulled her into me.

"Five more minutes" I said, and we continued to kiss in the kitchen until she got out of my clutches, and I had to finally go.

I got dressed in my signature black dress that I used to wear in Italy when work called and made my way to the company. It was lunch hour when I arrived and I figured she was out at the moment, I went to the reception and stood there as the woman looked at me.

"Can I help you with something?" she asked with a beaming smile that almost made me sick.

I lowered my shades as I squinted at her, "No, I can make my own way around" I said and was about to go to the elevator, but she stopped me.

"I'm sorry Miss, you can't enter without a reason, else I'll have to call security" she said as I looked around and noticed two guards cautiously making their way to me and I turned to the woman.

"First of all its Mrs, and if you want to keep your job and I mean all of you, you will let me go to *My office*" I said and showed my ID to her and her face dropped as she waved away the guards to back off, I smirked and went to the elevator. Having a powerful name definitely has it's perks.

I had two identifications, the business one I just used which is Mrs Persephone Black but on my personal one is, Black-Lopez since Luiza and I agreed on taking each other's names. I walked into the office, placed my bag on the desk and stood in front of the window overlooking the city. This feels horrible, I miss Italy. I got lost in my thoughts, thinking everyone is okay and if the business was working out like we hoped for, I didn't even hear the door open and the sound of footsteps before a voice called out to me.

I turned and my eyes landed on my sister, she had grown up so much and had a completely different look. The long hair gone to a shorter style to outline her features more. Her face full of life, her jawline, cheekbones and entire face looking sharper. Her eyes were still the same deep blue I always saw when I closed my eyes the first month in prison, wearing a suit that hugged her body perfectly as my gaze quickly shifted to the woman at her side.

Chestnut skin with darker hair hanging down her back, wearing a dress that fit her body perfectly. She seemed to be close with my sister by the proximity of their bodies and the side glances I didn't miss. I then returned my focus to River and the look of shock on her face, she definitely recognised me.

"I'm sorry can we help you?" the woman asked me, I focused my attention on her for a moment and laughed as I returned my gaze to River.

"River, you never introduced or told her about me" I said, and Rivers' mouth just dropped as she recognised my voice.

"Who are you?" the woman asked again, clearly talking for my sister as I turned my gaze to her and gave my best fake smile.

"Well pleasure to meet you darling, I'm Persephone Black, the rightful heir to this company."

Chapter Ten

CAITLYN

My eyes kept flicking between the sisters, I was fighting the urge to bite back at this woman's attitude, but I kept my thoughts to myself. I looked to River, and she was still in a state of shock, so I grabbed her shoulder to try and get her back to reality.

"River?" I asked and it was like I wasn't even here, I looked to Persephone, she raised an eyebrow and I frowned at her. "I'm going to go and leave you both to it" I said and began to leave but River's hand caught my wrist.

"You're staying" she said. I walked back and looked at her.

"This seems like a sensitive topic; I don't think I'm needed" I said and finally she turned her head to look at me.

"I need you here, so I don't rip her head off" her teeth were gritted, and I saw her free hand ball into a fist, I gave her a nod.

"Like you could even lay a hand on me" her sister was challenging River, and I don't know why but I felt like there would be some new information to come out today.

When River finally moved her feet, she moved a chair to her side for me to sit as her sister sat across the desk from us. I felt like I was going to get the full history of their family now, I was fighting so hard to not say something.

"Why did you never come back after your time?" River asked straight away as I watched Persephone turn her phone off and place it back in her bag.

"Let's not rush into questions, I'll give you the short version and then you can ask, capiche?" she said, and I raised my eyebrow at the sudden language change, she certainly hadn't lost the accent. River just nodded and let her start talking.

"So short version, dad was in deep with money fraud and told me to take the blame, so I did. I was committed to seven years but only did five, made some friends, moved to Italy, made a name for myself and now I'm back here. Questions?" she said, and I was surprised to learn about prison, and I could see River's brain trying to wrap her head around it all.

"So you're saying Dad lied to us and now you want me to believe you after you've been gone for 15 years!" she raised her voice and I saw the same heated anger within Persephone as well.

"You never visited me, I was your favourite, you said you'd come, and I was left alone River!" she shouted, and I saw the hurt in her eyes as they softened at River as did hers.

"Dad said you stole from us, that was it. How come you only did five years?" she wasn't listening but still asked her questions.

"First of all, I was glad to do only five, it wasn't even my sentence. Like I said I made friends, and the boss of that group got me out early, I figured the family didn't want me and the friends I made did, so I moved to Italy" she said, I looked to River, and she looked hurt but still held it together.

"In Italy for ten years! Doing what?" River asked and her voiced raised again.

"Doing dangerous work for dangerous people, but like all good things it came to an end. I run things now, and everything is level again, I came back for only one reason" she said and reached into her bag, brought out a folder and passed it to River.

River eyed her sister, then the folder and opened it, I leaned over and looked at the contract. My eyes scanned across it from the name of this company and to the bottom to the owner revealing Persephone's name.

"This means nothing!" River shouted, she stood up and slammed the contract on the desk.

"Yes it fucking does, I own all this, you can't break a contract! Shall we go see father and settle all of this?" Persephone now stood, her voice raised and echoed through the room, River stood frozen, probably not believing her sister would ever shout at her like that.

"Caitlyn, can you manage things here? I need to go home" she turned and asked me, I nodded not really wanting to argue. Both sisters stormed out of the building, and I walked back to my desk to see all eyes on me. Caleb came over quickly and leaned against my desk.

"Who was that? We all heard shouting" he asked, and I ran my hand through my hair, clearly feeling the stress.

"That was Persephone Black, the sister of River and apparently our true boss" I said, and he had a look of disbelief on his face. He quickly went back to work as soon as I asked, and I couldn't even focus on work as my mind was on River.

Work went by painfully slow, as I was leaving and walking to my car, my phone rang so as I got in the car I answered it seeing River's name flash on screen. "Hey, I was just about to text you, are you okay?" I was eager to find out what had happened after they left.

"Can I come over?" River asked and her voice was low, it sounded like she had been crying.

"Absolutely" I told her, we ended the call and I quickly drove home to be there before her.

But like always she beat me to it, as I parked and got out, I hurried to the front door and pulled her into a hug as she cried against my shoulder. "It's okay, it's okay" I told her, and we stood there for a moment before getting into the house. I made her sit on the couch as I made us hot cocoa, which seemed to help in any situation. I brought it to her, sat by her and she was just staring into nothing. I gave her time, remained silent as I put my mug down so did she, I took her hand gingerly and held it with mine.

"Do you want to talk about it?" I finally asked after a long silence, you could hear a pin drop by how quiet it got.

"My whole family is just one big fucking lie to me, I feel like the only people I can trust are my mother and Darcy" she said, and I moved closer to her.

"Well, that's not your whole family" I said trying to make it better but by her stoic look, I think I just made it worse.

"My father lied to us, he was found out for fraud and put the blame on my sister, then he worked me to the bone to run a company that isn't even mine, I'm just a joke to him. Then on the other hand, Persephone is basically a criminal mastermind in Italy but apparently that's all behind her, I just don't know what to believe anymore" she told me and I didn't know how to answer, I just wrapped my arm around her and hugged her as I felt her body shake again from crying.

"You'll figure this out, I know you will just give it time. What's happening at work tomorrow?" I asked her, I needed to know if she would be there.

"I'm not going, what's the point, it's not mine but you should still go" she looked up at me and I placed my hands onto her cheeks and brushed the tears away.

"Does Darcy know about any of this?" I asked her as she shook her head and wiped her face.

"No, but I need to tell her" she said and laid her head on my shoulder. She was so vulnerable then, this wasn't the hard ass, bitchy River right now. This was just a girl who got shown the reality of her life.

I kissed the top of her head and rubbed her arm with my hand as I kept quiet, saying anything right now would not be good. It would just make it worse, and I tend to do that. River stayed with me until it got late, and she had to go home, I stayed up for a couple hours after to see if she'd text and once I knew that wasn't going to happen I went to sleep, hoping I'd hear something tomorrow.

The next day came, and I went to work as usual but upon getting to my desk and going into River's office I was met with Persephone instead and I overheard her conversation as she turned to meet my eyes.

"I'll see you tonight for dinner, love you" she said and hung up her call. I raised an eyebrow but didn't ask questions.

"I didn't expect to see you here, I was hoping to see- "

"River, she'll arrive when she wants to" she cut me off and I was fighting the urge to talk back so badly but it still slipped out.

"Please don't interrupt me again, treat me with respect and you shall receive the same treatment, *capiche*?" I mocked her and that was a mistake as she strode towards me making me take steps back and into a wall where she cornered me.

"Don't play games with me sweetheart, I can do worse, don't provoke me" she said, and I rolled my eyes, but they instantly went wide when she grabbed my chin too hard and made me look at her. "Use your words, do you understand what I just said?" she asked as she stared right through me.

"Yes" I uttered, and she squeezed harder, what does this woman want, me on my knees begging? "Yes ma'am" I repeated, she released me and seemed pleased with that answer, who the heck am I working for?

I was at my desk the entire day and when I had work to do she simply sent it over as a message to my tablet. She never came out and I only got a glimpse of her when she left for lunch and that was it. I wondered how River was, when I took a small break, I got my phone out to text her wondering if she was okay and where she was. It didn't last long as my phone was snatched from me. I looked up and thankfully it was Caleb.

"Don't do that, I thought you were Miss pain in the ass" I whispered and snatched my phone back.

"Where's River?" he asked, and I began to wonder the same.

"I don't know, why?" I asked and he came around to my side.

"We all should have had meetings with her today but since she isn't here, we thought the new boss would do them but nothing all day" he said, and I looked to the rest to see them all looking over here.

"I'll go find out" I said made my way to the door, I knocked before entering and closed the door behind me to see her look up from her computer and gestured for me to sit down but I declined.

"Miss Black- "she raised her hand before I said anything else.

"Please, it's Mrs Black Lopez" she said, my mouth opened in shock, and I couldn't believe she was actually married.

"Sorry. As I was saying, all the employees out there had meetings with River today but that isn't happening, and they wondered if you were going to do them?" I told her, and she leaned back in her chair as her face twisted into confusion then she rolled her eyes.

"Does no one know how to read in this place" she groaned and got up and walked out of the office, I was hot on her heels so that when she stopped I bumped into her.

"I'm so sorry" I said and quickly backed away, but she grabbed my wrist and pulled me behind her not releasing her grip.

"So it's come to my attention that none of you can read here" she shouted out as all eyes fell on her and I felt very uncomfortable, but she held her ground.

"We had meetings today but obviously you had other plans" Michael said to her taking one for the team and I eyed him to not say anything else.

"I'd watch your next words very carefully Mr Evans" she said, and I was impressed that she learned everyone's name that fast.

"No, it's not right we want River back and not you, we have work to do and you were probably in there doing your nails" he said and everyone looked away and back to their screens as I looked away too and I felt Persephone tense up.

"You're right Mr Evans, how about you go back to your desk, collect your things and get out of my building" she said in a calm tone, and he was about to retort but she held her hand up. "Do not argue with me, get out you're fired" she said, and he didn't even argue, I guess the look on her face said it all. She waited till he grabbed what he needed and left the floor.

"As I was saying, it's clear mis-communication has happened, if you all look into your schedules on your computers which I have updated for all of you, you will see I have moved your meetings to not have them all in one day, they will happen from the start of next week. Any questions?" she finished off and no one answered so she went back into her office, dragging me with her and finally letting go.

"You have been here for four years, I trust you know this company well" she said, and I thought back to when River asked me the same question, I was about to nod and remembered to use words as to not be up against a wall again.

"Yes ma'am" I told her, and she nodded.

"Good, you can sit with me on these meetings and help decide what you think is best, got it?" she asked in quick succession, I nodded, and she quickly raised her eyebrow.

"Sorry, I'm still not used to it. Yes ma'am" I said quickly, turned to leave, walked into the door and then stumbled out feeling myself blush out of embarrassment.

The next month was sure to be interesting as I looked at the schedule and I just hoped River would contact me within that time frame.

Chapter Eleven

RIVER

As soon as we left the office, we drove separately with Persephone following me to the family home to finally get this contract business sorted out. As we parked, I looked over to her to see her taking in the house and I realised I had forgotten that she was taken away and missed out on so much. I just didn't understand why she hadn't come back, what had she found out that had made her stay away.

We walked in and the house maids told us where our parents were and upon entering the room and being announced my mother turned her head to smile at me and then her face dropped. First to confusion and then shock, it must be impossible for a mother to forget her daughters face. Persephone was also in shock from coming back home and seeing her parents for the first time in 15 years.

"Who's your friend River?" father asked as he took a quick glance my way to where I stood and motioned Persephone to talk. She finally snapped her eyes away from our mother to glare at the back of our fathers head.

"Missed me?" she said, as she moved more into the room. He slowly turned around, and the realisation washed over him, and I saw the fear in him, but he quickly collected himself.

"What are you doing here?" he asked, and I moved towards my mother who had now risen from her chair, and I held her hand to keep her from interfering.

"You mean, how was my time in prison that should have been yours?" she responded back to him, and I saw her fists clenched.

"What is she talking about?" my mother asked, and my father looked to her then back to Persephone.

"You need to leave" he said to Persephone, his teeth gritted together as his knuckles turned white as he clenched the glass he held.

"We need answers and the truth!" Persephone spat out as she slammed the contract down on the table and moved it towards him.

I watched his face change through a series of emotions and finally fear was stuck on his face as he swallowed and looked up to Persephone. "How did you get this? What have you done?" he asked as the fear settled in him, he took a step back from her and I watched as she ran a hand through her long hair and paced back and forth.

"You left me to fight for myself in that hell hole, I had to do what was needed but don't worry you won't have to answer or talk to the Don anymore" she said to him, and I was confused who this Don character was. My father was caught like a deer in headlights, he didn't know where to look or what to say.

"Where is he?" he asked fearing the answer and I gripped my mother's hand more.

"Dead and buried. I saved the love of my life from that man, now you're going to answer some questions and finally tell the truth, like the loyal man I thought you were" she said and he finally gave in and sat down at the table as did she, my mother and I walked over to do the same. I looked at Persephone's hand to notice she had a wedding ring and also a signet ring, but I didn't recognise the emblem.

The conversation went back and forth and was not really getting to the point, so we decided to go from the start all of those years ago, from what really happened, no more lies needed to be said to put a wedge between us, but trust was going to be hard to gain back.

Father started and told us about what had happened, that he 'borrowed' money from the company he worked for and got caught doing so. He made Persephone take the blame for a price at the end of her sentence, he didn't realise it would be for seven years and worked hard to make a name for himself so she would have something at the end of it and continue his legacy. He had met with this Don after receiving a very cold message asking for a meeting, where the contract for the business was written up and in time Persephone would take hold of it, but it never happened.

On Persephone's side of the story, she mentioned how her sentence was cut short by two years due to making friends in prison who were connected to the Don. He got her out early and prepared to have her live her life in Italy. Everything was going smooth until she had to kill people which has haunted her; I saw her hand shake like she was reliving it and holding a weapon. Then she met a woman who she fell in love with, one day it just got too much and people she worked for found out her love worked for a rival mafia family so they were going to kill her and when the Don had a knife to her throat and forced her to shoot her lover, Persephone changed target and shot the Don. Over the years, everything changed for that family, they escaped the mafia life and entered the business trade to have something they could be proud of, but I still saw the sadistic side in my sister, the small smile she got when she told us she killed the Don, it was like I didn't know her anymore.

Silence fell over us all and father was rereading the contract, my mother had moved to sit by Persephone to hold her hand, I was just confused and knew Darcy would need to know about all of this.

"The contract can't be broke, I made it necessary to have no loop holes in it, River I'm so sorry" he finally said, my head snapped to him as I felt the pain in my chest.

"So I have nothing, I worked so hard for nothing!" I finally rose from my chair and held up my hand as I saw my mother attempt to calm me.

"It's done, we can't change that, you can still work for the company just not as CEO" he said, and I ran a hand over my face, slammed my fist down after hearing that insult to work as less than a CEO and began to make my way to the door.

"Where are you going?" my mother asked me, I stopped and turned to look at her.

"If you have forgotten, you do have another daughter who deserves to hear all this, I'll be the one to tell her since she is the only one I can rely on right now" I said and then made my way out of the house. As I got in the car, my hands were shaking and I had just lost everything I had worked so hard for, I didn't know what to do.

I called Caitlyn to go see her after work and told her most of what I remember, I was on autopilot and not really remembering much but my sister is now dangerous, although she said she had changed I couldn't believe it.

After being at Caitlyn's I went home to see Darcy and Sasha in the lounge eating pizza, I made my presence known and Sasha noticed I wasn't myself as she helped me sit and made sure I was sane.

I couldn't hold it back and I silently sobbed as she held me, and Darcy was getting worried, and I let it all out. I had to tell her everything I had learnt, she needed to know. I was not going to follow his footsteps and lie to people, from experience it solved nothing. She didn't have much to say since she didn't really remember from her being so young, but I found an old photo album and as we went through, things were falling into place, and she was slowly understanding but it didn't change anything for her.

I spent the night alone, figuring I didn't have work tomorrow since it's been taken over, I really had nothing to do. But with the new day I took my time in the shower figuring out what I needed to do. I could go back to the company and work in a lower position but that just didn't fit right with me. Did she even have more qualifications than me for this job, I wasn't stupid enough to cross her but there has to be some sort of silver lining here.

I tried to call or text Caitlyn but no answer, she must be watched by Persephone, I decided to see if I could find anything on her former boss, Don Bruno Orsini but just as I thought nothing came up, for a mafia boss it would be private.

I let the days pass me by to my dismay but eventually at the end of a long week, I decided to go back to the company and upon entering, it seemed like I was missed. I walked out onto the main floor and everyone's eyes were on me and the smiles greeted me as well, but it seemed we had lost someone. I made my way to Caleb seeing as Caitlyn was nowhere to be seen either.

"Where's Michael?" I asked him wondering what I had missed in the last week.

"She fired him for talking back and saying she did nothing so that department has been cold" he said, I nodded, finally I pick up my pace and walk through *my* office to see her in *my* chair at *my* desk and Caitlyn sitting next to her as they worked.

I cleared my throat and Caitlyn quickly rose to her feet, but Persephone placed a hand on her lower back to make her sit again, she got up and moved around to me.

"Took you long enough to come back dear sister" she said with that stupid smirk on her face, and I looked to Caitlyn to see her head lowered as I stared back at my sister.

"Is this what you are doing now, setting fear into anyone who gets in your way?" I asked her knowing how people felt already just by them missing me which had never happened before.

"It's not my fault no one has a strong mind for this work, which by the way, I've made some changes and let's just say it's working better" she said, and she motioned for me to walk around the desk to see what she was talking about.

"Connecting this with my work in Italy will be good for both sides, trust me, we are down a department but that can be easily replaced" she said, and I realised I had to take a shot to get back what I worked hard for.

"I'll take it" I said not really thinking clearly and she gave me a stern look, but Caitlyn had confusion wash over her face.

"I know it better than anyone, it's one I worked hard on, I'll take it, if you will allow me?" I asked her and I was not going to beg if she denied me. I hated this but that department was the highest of the rest and would ruin us to lose it. Persephone gave a small nod.

"Ok, don't disappoint me" she said, and I resisted to roll my eyes as I walked out of the office and went to Mr Evans' old desk. The other employees gave me all a confused look as I set myself up.

"Don't worry, it won't be for long, let's just work" I told them, and they all gave a cautious nod and resumed work. Lunch came faster than expected and once everyone left I waited for Caitlyn and caught her on the way to the elevator, we walked in silence until we were outside.

"Can we have lunch together?" I asked her once we were alone, she gave me a nod and she followed me to my car. The drive was quiet, but I chose the sushi place where we had been before. As we entered and took our seats, I decided to break the silence.

"Is everything okay? Has Persephone been giving you a hard time?" I asked her and she glanced at me over the menu before placing it down.

"I don't know how to feel after what you told me about the criminal shit" she said in a low whisper so no one would hear us. The thought had crossed my mind, but I didn't see how it would affect Caitlyn at all.

"What do you mean? You have nothing to worry about" I told her, but she shot me a cold look that I had never seen before.

"Don't I? If I get involved with you, I'm risking myself since you are connected to her, I just don't know anymore" she said, and I was starting to see two thoughts here and didn't know which one she was thinking off.

"Involved with who, me or her?" I asked her and she didn't answer but that was more than enough. She wanted this with me and now because my sister has a dark past she wanted nothing to do with me. I needed answers from Persephone, it might still be risky to be with Caitlyn, but we have to try, what is life without some risks.

Lunch was eaten in silence and as soon as we got back to the office, I went to where she was, not even knocking just walking in to see another woman sitting with her on the couch across the room. She stood quickly as to answer to what I just walked in on.

"Do you know how to knock before entering?" she asked me and I rolled my eyes and looked at the woman on the couch, she gave me a simple smile. She seemed to be around Persephone's age and had long dark brown hair and wore simple clothes of jeans and a blouse.

"Who's this?" I asked not wanting to jump to conclusions, but I had a guess.

"This is my wife, Luiza. Luiza this is River, my sister" Persephone said, and she got up and walked to me to shake my hand which I gave.

"Nice to meet you" I said, and she nodded as Persephone wrapped up their talk giving her a kiss as she left the office and then Persephone focused on me. She seemed more relaxed when her wife was around, a softer side of her. When she left, that quickly diminished, and her cold exterior was back, and she looked at me with the same blank stare.

"Does the family or myself have anything to worry about, like your past coming back?" I asked and I watched her closely to see any falter in her expression, but nothing came.

"You have nothing to worry about" she said and then a thought came to me that appeared when I spoke to Darcy, when I told her about all this.

"Did you or anyone related to you have anything to do with Darcy's kidnapping last year?" I asked her and her demeanour shifted, did she know about that or was she part of it. She wouldn't go that far to hurt the family right?

"I heard about that, a woman I had met in prison, she was watching me, and mentioned you and Darcy. I threatened her the best I could, but she got out and had been watching the family for a while, she planned it. But I'm glad Darcy was saved" she told me, and I just nodded, she seemed honest in her answer and that raised another question.

"What happened to the woman?" I had to ask and by her smirk I could already guess, "Do you gain pleasure from killing?" I asked out of the blue and her smirk dropped, and she looked away from me as she bit her lip.

"At first no but people deserve it. It haunts you though, I fall into a dark place and just get stuck there before I'm pulled back" she said and it was almost a whisper, I began to think that her wife must be the anchor for her.

I ended the conversation as there was another employee that came to speak to her, so I left the office. I hovered by Caitlyn's desk, and she gave me a smile and I took that to power me through the day. We'll get back on track in time.

Chapter Twelve

CAITLYN

A month has passed by since Persephone had come to the company and taken over. River had been working as head of one of the departments, but I could see it was not what she really wanted. She was trying to form a conversation with me whenever she gets the chance, but I just can't stay around her for long.

My feelings for River are still strong for her but all the information about her sister just made me not want to get involved. What if River becomes a target then that makes me a target, I just don't want danger and drama from it all. Even though Persephone has seemingly come away from that she could still have loose strings and connections.

It was the start of a new week and after meetings and differences being argued we were finally ready to open a new nightclub, a project that River had concluded after taking over Michael's work. I was invited by Persephone to attend since she agreed that I had been a big help towards finishing it. I never mentioned what happened in San Deigo to anyone, but Caleb, Conor and Damon and I wasn't planning on it. So when she asked what had happened at the last meeting and why it didn't have a good ending, I lied and just said it was creative differences. She didn't seem to believe me but didn't push it.

I was putting the final touches of my outfit together when I heard a knock on the door and quickly made my way to open it to see Caleb and Conor since they were also attending the opening.

"You look beautiful Caitlyn" Conor gushed, and I did a small twirl for them as I looked at them both.

"You both look handsome as always, but let's get going, we are already late" I said, and we made the quick drive to the nightclub.

As we entered, the place was lit up by bright colours of purple and blue. A long table was set up with food from different countries and a bar with a range of drinks from cocktails to beer. I looked around and spotted River and Persephone at once with a woman who I assumed was her wife as she had her arm hooked through Persephone's, having a conversation for once. I watched them for a while and noticed them both smiling and at one point laughing, and I asked myself if things were getting better between them both after a while River excused herself and walked away as I made that my attempt to walk over to Persephone.

"I made it" I announced as she looked me up and down and smiled.

"So you have, and you look amazing. This is my wife Luiza" she introduced, and I shook her hand and introduced myself. They both matched each other perfectly as a beautiful couple, Persephone was the moon, the dark one while Luiza was the sun, the light in their relationship, I felt envy only because I wanted that one day.

"This place is going to be packed soon, and everyone will be having a good time, you've worked well this month, you deserve to have fun" she told me, I nodded, and she quickly grabbed my chin to look at her as I kept forgetting her rule. She slowly used her thumb to wipe the corner of my mouth probably fixing my lipstick and then she looked into my eyes. Luiza didn't seem to mind as if this were a behaviour she was used to witness.

"I um, I'll try to have a good time" I tell her and she nods accepting my answer, drops my chin and leads her wife away to talk to the people who made this project happen and I had a moment to calm myself down after that encounter as I made my way to the bar for a much needed drink.

As the party got into full swing it indeed got very busy, people stood like sardines in a can, but I managed to keep to the outskirts of people talking, some people grabbing my attention for congratulations but that was all. I had lost Persephone and River in the sea of people as well as Caleb and Conor, so I was looking for them, but I was grabbed by the wrist and pulled to a secluded area. My breath hitched as I came face to face with none other than Reginald Huntington. I tried to run away but he grabbed me and pinned me against the wall with his hand.

"Let me go!" I shouted at him, and he placed his hand over my mouth to silence me, but I bit his hand, and he changed tactic to hold me by the throat instead so I couldn't scream. My eyes widened in fear.

"You are surely a hard one to find but I finally got you all alone. I have been watching you" he said, I frowned, and my eyes darted around to try and see someone I recognised.

"So you remember me?" I managed to ask as I felt his grip loosen and I quickly caught my breath. My eyes looked at his face and that disgusting smirk was plastered on his face.

"At that meeting months ago it didn't cross my mind, but afterwards, of course, how could I forget the soft skin, curvy hips and plump lips" he taunted as his hand grazed my thigh and I pushed him back the best I could.

"Get the hell away from me" I spat at him, and his hand now roughly grabbed my face, I winced at the pain.

"You need to learn respect Caitlyn and I can show you that for sure" he threatened, and that old feeling came back to my chest, and I was finding it hard to breathe.

"Is there a problem here?" a voice said, my eyes snapped to the person over his shoulder, and I was so happy to see Persephone. Reginald removed his hand and stepped back from me.

"Just catching up is all" he said but she didn't buy it. She didn't even look at him and kept her eyes on me.

"Did he hurt you?" she asked, and I didn't expect that. I shook my head but kept my words direct for her.

"He didn't have a chance to" I said and gave him a glare as he clenched his fists as she turned her eyes to him.

"I suggest you leave, because as far as I'm aware, you were not invited" she threatened, and I could hear the disdain in her voice, but he just smirked and laughed in her face. He turned away and as his laughter faded he looked back at her and was about to slap her, but she caught his wrist and her face contorted into pure fury.

"I gave you a chance, come near her again and I'll kill you myself" she finished the conversation and twisted his arm behind his back escorting him personally out of the building as I kept my pace behind her until River cut me off.

"Caitlyn, what happened, did he hurt you?" she asked worry clear on her face. I shook my head but pushed past her as I saw security finally drag him out and Persephone made her way back to me. I don't know what came over me, but I threw my arms around her in a hug, if she hadn't come in time I don't want to think of the outcome. She wrapped an arm around me and ushered me away from the party into a separate room. I felt another presence come in and pulled away to see River there as well.

"How do you know Reginald Huntington?" Persephone asked and I looked between her and River, I didn't like this at all.

"You don't need to answer" River said until Persephone faced her.

"I think she does, if I hadn't walked by who knows what would have happened? So how do you know him?" she asked again as she faced me. I sat down on the couch in the room and now I felt forced to say it, so I did, I didn't look at either of them but told them what happened when I was 15 keeping my head down.

"Oh my god" River breathed out as she sat by me.

"I'm going to kill him" Persephone finally said, and my head shot up towards her.

"Please do not kill anyone, I couldn't bear knowing that, you can't just say stuff like that" I said and stood up from the couch, I felt River hold my hand.

"She didn't mean it, she said all that stuff was behind her" River said and then stood up with me.

"I can't stand people like that, but I understand your worry. If he comes near you or does anything to you again when we aren't close, you need to tell me, can you do that?" she asked me, I gave a simple nod, and she accepted that as an answer.

"Persephone, do you remember what we spoke about earlier?" River asked Persephone and this must have been what had made them both smile. She looked between us both and then her eyes landed on our hands that were still together.

"I assure you" she said and gave the both of us a smile and left the room. I turned to River with a curious look, and she smiled at me.

"What was that about?" I asked her and she played it cool until I pulled her closer.

"I told Persephone that we may have feelings for each other, but I wanted to know if we are safe to be in a relationship even with her past or the company. She told me how she and her wife met, it was not the same circumstances but I understand her message. Life is too short to not take chances" she said, but I was still confused because I didn't know the whole story.

"What do you- "

"Will you go out with me?" she cut me off and I was taken aback as I didn't expect that, "I'm crazy about you and you are on my mind from when I wake up until the moment I fall asleep" she tells me and I can feel my cheeks heat up from the compliment. "Just give me a chance" she whispered as she got closer to me, I felt her breath on my face.

"Yes" I whispered, and she smiled as she cupped my cheeks with her hands and pulled me into a kiss. Even though we had kissed before, this felt like the first time, I enjoyed her soft lips upon mine and how gently she led the kiss.

It wasn't a simple kiss, as I kissed back we let our feelings show it was obvious how much we needed this. As I placed my hands around her waist, she pulled away and then let her thumb brush across my bottom lip.

"You're so beautiful" she whispered to me, and I smiled at her.

"You're such a sap" I teased, and she laughed with me as we shared one more kiss before we rejoined the party where we found Caleb and Conor, and they noticed the change between River and I as she still had her arm wrapped tightly around my waist.

"So you two are together now?" Conor asked us, the hope in his eyes.

"We are taking it slow" I said, and he came to my side for a hug then Caleb did the same.

Hours later I could feel the fatigue come over me and I was ready for bed, Caleb and Conor had already left but I stayed as I wanted to spend more time with River but as I sat down for a break I could feel my eyes drop.

"Do you want me to take you home?" I heard River's voice in front of me and I didn't open my eyes, but I just nodded. She helped me up and walked us out of the club and to her car where she helped me get in. My head sank against the window, and I fell asleep. Before I knew it I was being shaken awake and I opened my eyes to see us parked outside my house.

"Where are your keys, so I can help you inside?" she asked, I passed her my bag, and went to sleep again. I was in and out of sleep as I heard my front door open and close, River carried me up the stairs and then plonked me onto the bed.

"River my shoes" I whined and lifted my foot in the air.

I heard her chuckle as she moved along the room, and I felt her hand hold my foot.

"So high maintenance" she teased as she undid my shoe and placed my leg down to do the other and then placed my shoes on the floor.

"Are you going to sleep in your dress?" she asked me, and I shook my head.

"Leave the room and I'll undress" I said, and I heard her huff, but she left the room, and I smiled as I opened my eyes, wide awake, and smirked at my impressive plan. I got out of the dress, took my bra off for comfort, put on a simple tee, got into bed and called for River again. She walked into the room and knelt at the side of my bed as I had my eyes closed again.

"Are you going to be okay alone?" she asked as she stroked my head which started to make me sleepy.

"Can you stay?" I asked and opened my eyes to see her looking at me.

"If you want me to" she whispered and I nodded, she got up, took off her shoes, tie and shirt and laid above the sheets on the other side of the bed. I turned over so I was facing her.

"Get under the sheets" I told her, and she shook her head but gave in and I instantly snuggled up to her as she wrapped an arm around me.

"Now get some sleep" she said and kissed my head. I nodded and let sleep take me.

The next couple of weeks went flying by and River and me were stable in our secret relationship, we would go on dates out of town to not get caught by people we worked with. At work we kept it professional but would steal glances at each other and I could say, in a safe environment, that we were girlfriends, and I couldn't have been happier.

I was still cautious whenever I was out, fearing that Reginald was back in town, and he were to find me at any moment, but I was trying not to think about it too much. I walked out of the elevator onto the top floor, passed by the cubicles where I gave a quick glance to River before I knocked on the office door. When I walked in to give Persephone a folder of documents I stopped in my tracks as I saw someone sitting opposite her.

She had a dark undercut with blonde highlights throughout which fit her olive skin well. She wore navy pants with ankle boots and a polo shirt buttoned up to the top. She had a watch on her left wrist, a chain around the right matching the one around her neck. She had earrings and a noticeable slit through her eyebrow as she looked my way, I was met with dark eyes.

"I'm so sorry, I didn't know you had company" I apologised and bowed my head as a form of respect.

"It's fine, pass them here" Persephone said and held her hand out, I was too stunned to move but when I heard her fingers click I remembered what I had to do and gave the folder to her. I looked at her friend who was already looking at me.

"You sure know how to hire them, Black" the woman said, and her voice had the Italian accent pouring from it, so this must be a friend she made over there.

"Eyes off, she's taken by my sister" Persephone said making me snap my head to her and blush.

"Persephone!" I argued but she gave me a blank stare.

"Am I wrong?" she asked, and I shook my head and looked away feeling embarrassed.

"I'm just looking, no harm in that. Pleasure to meet you, I'm Addison Remington but you can call me Remy" she said and held out her hand to me and I took a moment to admire her tattoos as I shook her hand.

"I'm Caitlyn, you have some beautiful artwork on your arms" I complimented as I released her hand.

"Thank you, I'm covered" she said with a wink, I smiled and looked away as I blushed which made her laugh.

"Ew, stop it" Persephone said and handed the files back to me, "Thank you" she said, and I took them and left the office. I placed down the documents as I sat down trying to hide my amusement. An hour after meeting Remy she finally left the office and as she was about to leave she stopped at my desk.

"We should meet sometime for a drink" she said and passed me a piece of paper that had her number written on it, I looked at her and raised my eyebrow as she held her hands up in defence. "As a friend, I assure you" she said, and I placed the paper down.

"I'll think about it" I said, and she nodded taking that as a yes and left the office. A moment later, River came to my desk, crouched down and pretended to ask something work related.

"Who was that?" she asked in a whisper while showing me papers with scribbles on them.

"Friend of your sister's from Italy, she gave me her number to meet up sometime" I told her, and she grabbed my hand under the desk.

"Does she know you're taken?" she asked, and I smiled at her.

"Persephone made it very clear, don't worry" I told her, and she relaxed but I could tell that she still didn't like it. "I only have eyes for you, you don't have to worry" I assured her, and it seemed to get through to her. "Now go back to work" I ordered, and she got up, grabbed the papers and went back to her desk.

Even though Persephone instilled fear into every fibre of me, I do believe she protects her family and friends no matter what it takes and people listen to her. Like just then in her office, she could have let her friend flirt with me, but she shot her down instantly and her friend seemed to not press it and listened to her. I'm starting to think Persephone really made a name for herself in the past and that was starting to scare me more but heightened my respect for her.

I invited River over for dinner after work and she agreed instantly, but before I could cook anything I had to make a run to the store to pick up food for dinner. As I walked down the isles I caught the eye of someone that I knew I'd see sometime soon. He looked my way and gave me a smile, but I knew what was going through his head. I continued shopping trying to ignore him, but he caught up to me down the dairy isle.

"Are you following me?" he asked as he stood next to me acting like he was a normal customer.

"You were told to not come near me" I told him and took a step away, but he matched it coming closer.

"You think I'm scared of that whore" he said, and I snapped my head to him, who the hell did he think he was?

"Don't you dare call her that" I started to raise my voice, but he moved his face towards mine.

"Or what? You seriously think you can threaten me, I make the rules here" he said and looked in my basket then back at me, "Enjoy your meal" he said and then walked away from me. I dropped the basket and quickly made my way out of the store and leaned against the wall to calm myself down. My hands were shaking, and sweat was beading on my forehead.

I managed to get out my keys and drove myself back home, but my thoughts were clouded by what had happened. Do I call Persephone or River? Shit River! I was at home sitting on the couch waiting for her, I kept looking from the door to the clock and back again until she knocked on the door and came in.

"Caitlyn?" she called out and walked to the lounge where I was sitting down, and she quickly saw that I wasn't in a good state. "What happened baby?" she asked and wrapped an arm around me.

"I went to the store to buy food for tonight, but I didn't get it" I told her, and she rubbed my back giving me time to say what actually happened. "Reginald has been following me, he was at the store and threatened me again and he called Persephone a vile name, I hate this, do I call her?" I asked River finally looking at her.

"I'm not going to tell you what to do, but whatever you decide, I'll support you" she said, and I took my time to think about this, Persephone could do serious damage, but it would end. I made the call.

I didn't tell her the details, just that she had to come over quickly and she agreed to it. It took 30 minutes until she knocked on the door and came inside the house. I noticed she was dressed down in sweats and a hoodie, but she still looked good.

"What happened?" she asked as she sat opposite River and me.

"Reginald found me at the store, he came close and threatened me and he called you a whore" I told her and felt sick again, so I slowly sipped the water I had next to me to calm me down.

"I've been called worse. Do you want me to take care of this?" she asked me, and I still didn't know the answer, so I asked her a simple question.

"Will all this stop?" She leaned forward and took my hands in hers.

"The memories probably won't but you will never see him again, I'll take care of it" she said and brought my hands up and kissed them.

"Just don't let me know about it?" I asked, and she nodded. She got up and kissed mine and River's cheek then left. I laid my head against River as she held me in her arms. Did I do the right thing, or have I just done more damage to the situation?

Chapter Thirteen

PERSEPHONE

When I left Caitlyn's after hearing what had happened I made some calls to friends of mine to meet tomorrow at my home, it was time to end this the only way I was good at.

The next morning came, and I told Luiza the plan of what was going to happen, she was not happy, but she was persuaded by my words. As we finished our coffee, a knock at the door came and I was greeted by Remy, Janet and Martinez. The girls had come over from Italy for vacation, but they were ready for any request I had.

I told them who Reginald was and what he had been doing, I laid out all of the documents I had on him. Ever since that night at the club I had done research while at work to find out as much as I could about him and he is one of the worst. He had good lawyers to get him out of anything but that would all end soon.

So, I explained the plan to the girls, they were going to infiltrate his business to find information where they could and when we had something, I would bring Martinez along to hack into the accounts and leave them with nothing. He had four major businesses in California but hitting one would also damage the rest. We only had to destroy one and when we got him, I'd convince him to sign everything over to me.

The plan was set, and the girls left the house to get started. I was about to go upstairs to start my work, but Luiza grabbed my arm.

"We're doing this together" she said, and I gave her a look, I didn't want her involved, I had to keep her safe, but I also knew her better than that.

"Luiza" I tried to argue but she raised an eyebrow. People think I am intimidating, and I have more power than I would like but behind these walls, I'm submissive to my wife.

"I'm coming and that's final" she told me and grabbed me by the shirt pulling me into a kiss.

"Yes ma'am" I said, and we headed upstairs to prepare for what was to come.

A couple days passed until the first stage of the plan was a success and then all we had to do was follow him. It was late at night, Luiza and I were in a black SUV outside of the company where he was today. I had Remy using a drone to track his car in case we lost it, and I had Janet and Martinez in a transit van behind us.

"Okay, he is leaving now, get ready" Remy told us through our earpieces. As he got into his car and drove off, I left a two car space and then followed as did Janet soon after. We kept the distance and lost him at one point but were back on track quickly. As he pulled into his driveway, I drove past it to not cause suspicion as Janet and Martinez parked opposite his house and got out dressed as maintenance workers and pretended to be fixing a circuit board nearby. I went around the block and parked in the next street before we got out and walked along the path, keeping to shadows, we saw his home across the road.

"How's it looking Remy?" I asked her and I held Luiza's hand as she rubbed her thumb across my hand.

"It's calm so far, he has no guards, nobody else is there, he is all alone" she said, and this couldn't be that easy. We moved up the road to where the other two were as we had planned to cut the power to his home.

"How's it going?" I asked and Martinez pointed to his house as we looked.

"And we have… lights out" she said as we saw the place go dark.

"Get ready" I said, and we all put on gloves as Luiza and I ran onto his property, Janet would follow in the car we arrived in, and Martinez drove the transit onto his driveway.

We broke open the front door as we heard a gun click and the first shot was fired. I dove forward and Luiza stepped back outside. She gave me a look and shut the door as I rounded the corner and got out my pocket knife.

"I know who it is, you fucking bitch!" he fired another shot and I saw the bullet penetrate the wall in front of me as I saw his foot come into view. I stabbed the knife into his foot and as he cried out he used the blunt end of the shotgun to hit me in the head luckily missing the sensitive spot to knock me out. I was dazed though as I felt him place his foot on my back and I felt the barrel of the gun against my head.

"I've had enough of this" he shouted but another gunshot made him drop his gun and he fell to the ground holding his shoulder. I turned my head to see Luiza holding a gun as she came to me and pulled me away. I blinked rapidly and focused my attention on the situation, thinking I could have been dead right now if not for Luiza.

I got up and rubbed my head, I grabbed the shotgun and hit him hard in the head to knock him out. The four of us carried his body into the transit van and drove him to a secluded place.

I had found an abandoned mill that had a basement, we drove there and carried his body downstairs, sat him in a chair and tied him up only keeping his hands free.

"You got this?" Janet asked and I nodded to her as she and Martinez left leaving Luiza and me to finish this. I slapped him and threw cold water on his face as he coughed and woke up.

"You'll fucking pay!" he began to curse, but he stopped as Luiza held a gun to his head. "What do you want?" he asked me, and I moved a table in front of him with all the documents he had to sign to hand over everything, even his home.

"Just sign these and I'll make it quick, take your time and so will I" I threatened, and he didn't seem to buy it but still read over the contracts as I started a timer. After he had read them I looked at the timer to see it read 30 minutes and I looked at him.

"You think I'll just sign over everything?" he asked, and he seemed cocky as he found this funny.

"If you want your son to have kids in the future, I suggest you do" his face dropped as I mentioned his family and he shakily grabbed the pen and began to sign each document. I knew someone who could forge handwritings and would fake a note for his sudden disappearance.

After he signed the contracts I took them away as Luiza hit the gun against his head causing him pain and then began to tie his arms to his body so he couldn't grab us.

"I signed them, just let me go" he pleaded but I looked at him with a blank stare.

"You find it normal to touch young girls and think it's not wrong" I asked, and he didn't answer me. I looked at the timer, "40 minutes, any final words" I asked and waited, and he looked me dead in the eye.

"I'd do it again" and that was all I had to hear as I grabbed a crowbar and slammed it into his jaw, and he screamed as his blood coated my face.

"Let's have some fun with this" I grabbed a knife and slapped his face to look at me and I jammed the knife into his kneecap as he screamed out and began to cry as I twisted the knife and popped his kneecap out of place.

"This is what happens when you are a sick fuck" I told him and watched as Luiza grabbed pliers, moved to him, grabbed his hands and used the tool to pull off each of his fingernails and each scream was music to my ears.

We each took turns beating him with different tools, breaking bones until he lost consciousness to the blood loss and Luiza and I had his blood covering us. I checked his pulse, and it was slow but still present. I grabbed the gun and pointed it at him, and I knew my hand was shaking, Luiza placed her hand over mine. I looked to her, and she knew what was going through my head. I let my finger pull the trigger before the gun fell from my hand, she grabbed my hand and pulled me into a hug. I knew what I just did, and I knew what was to come.

She pulled away and held my face with both hands as she wiped the blood on my face across my cheek. "I love you" she said as she pulled me into a kiss, and I kissed her back and I backed her against the wall as we deepened the kiss. I started to attack her neck with kisses and bites until she held my hips and stopped me.

"As much as I want this to happen amore mia, I'd rather do it in the safety of our home and not with the scent of decay settling in" Luiza told me, and I looked around realising she was right. I nodded and we began to clean up, we burned everything, the body, the tools and our clothes and then got changed into different ones. We got rid of all the evidence and left the basement. I called the girls thanking them as we drove home.

That night as I was in the bathroom getting ready for bed, I splashed my face with water and looked at myself in the mirror. I couldn't recognise myself once more, I looked down to see my hand shaking again so I grabbed it and massaged it to stop. I walked into the bedroom to see Luiza reading a book, as soon as she saw me she opened her arms, and I walked over to lay in her arms as she read silently.

"I love you too" I whispered, and I knew she heard it. She placed a kiss upon my head and continued to read. "You're not going to leave me are you?" I asked quietly and she closed the book, puts it down and laid down next to me holding herself up on her elbow.

"Never in a million years" she said and kissed my exposed shoulder, I reached forward and tucked a strand of hair behind her ear.

"How did I get so lucky?" I wondered as I placed my hand on her cheek as she turned her face to kiss my hand.

"You got lucky by walking into the correct pool hall all of those years ago" she replied, and I smiled at her as she repositioned herself to wrap her arms around me, and I laid my head on her chest and eventually went to sleep.

I didn't show up to the company for a week as I was still coping with what had happened with Reginald. The news didn't mention much about his death. I had a forger use his signature to fake his handwriting to write a convincing note to his family and that was it. I sat at my dining table with the documents he signed sprawled all over it. I was so focused that I didn't hear Luiza call me at first and when I turned to look at her I also saw River.

"I'll leave you both to talk" she said as she winked at me and walked away leaving me with River. I let River walk in and she looked over the documents.

"You did it then?" she asked, and I nodded beginning to massage my hand.

"Everyone at work is getting suspicious about your weeklong absence, people fear you, but you are good at your job, you need to come back and be the CEO I know you are" she said and surprised me, I scoffed and stood up from the chair.

"I only did that to spite you, you clearly know what you are doing as well" I told her as when I had started there I had been really surprised by how successful she was.

"But you have the connections across the world" she told me, and I waved my hand at her.

"It only goes so far" I said, and she looked over a couple more documents.

"Look, I still don't know what is happening between us, but I believe we can work through it. I'm sorry that I never came to see you, truthfully I was scared to see you like that, you are my big sister and then I learned you're a criminal, knowing that is now a lie changes all that. But this mafia shit, you need to promise me right now, it's all done" she told me, and I finally understood River more. She was willing to let go of the past and my mistakes but was I?

"It's part of my life I'm never going to escape that but I tried my hardest to steer what I gained away from that and I did, I'd never go back to the mafia system only when necessary like with Reginald, I can't promise it will be the last but I'll try, can you accept that?" I asked her, and she took a moment to think and then approached me holding out her hand.

"I can if you can?" she offered, and I took her hand before pulling her into a much needed hug.

"I missed you so much Persephone" she said into my body, and I held her tighter.

"So did I River" I responded and held her for a moment longer before pulling away.

"So, the company, how about us running it together, we both have the education and great ideas. Sisters running the business together?" River offered to me, and it didn't seem so bad.

"Okay yeah, that doesn't sound that horrible" I told her making her laugh.

"Great so Monday you better show up" she told me, but I had one small request for her.

"River, can I ask a favour?" I asked her and she nodded to let me continue. "Can you ask Darcy if she would be willing to see me?" I asked and River took time to think.

"I can ask her, yeah" she said and that was all I wanted, it would be nice to have both sisters back, but we would see how Darcy felt. River left not long after and I began to gather up the papers knowing it was going to change going forward.

Chapter Fourteen

RIVER

The day after I went to see Persephone to make sure she was alright, I could see she wasn't, even after our civil conversation. At times her hand would shake, and her eyes looked distant. I had no idea what she had done and didn't even want to think about it.

I went home straight afterwards to see Darcy and asked her about seeing Persephone as it would be nice to have the three of us back together. I found her in her room and had a lengthy talk with her. She had questions about the family and Persephone's past. I only explained what I could and told her that she'd have to ask herself if she wanted to and she agreed to see Persephone soon so that was some good news from all this that has happened.

I went to work the next day and quickly made my way to the office to make sure she showed up and as I walked in, I had the biggest smile on my face when I saw Persephone was back.

"You're late" she said to me, but a smile broke out on her face.

"Don't even start with that" I said and closed the door behind myself.

"I've sent a message to the heads for a meeting to explain to them what is happening with the change" she said, and I nodded, I also rearranged the office and brought in another desk so we could each have our own, the employees were confused but they have to wait for the announcement.

We had time to sort out what we had to discuss and then went to the conference room for the meeting, seeing the employees and Caitlyn ready we began. We started with announcing that Persephone and I would be running the company together and it would be better since she had connections out of this country that would come in handy. We announced a new department which would be real estate and that we would be hiring for that position and a new head for the nightclub department as well. We discussed new project ideas we had and to have each department work hard for the future. Then we had one final announcement and Persephone let me take it from here.

"Now this didn't take a lot of thought and I think all of you would agree to this, but we have decided that Caitlyn, is going to be promoted to COO" I announced and the look of shock on her face would have been great to capture as everyone around her agreed that it was the right choice, telling her to take it or already congratulating her.

"It involves more work but no more then you already do for the company, you would be a great addition to have by our side" I added on, and she held back her tears but agreed and jumped to hug myself and Persephone not caring about who was watching. We had more to discuss with her but that could be done in private.

After concluding the meeting and everyone leaving for an early lunch, Persephone allowed me to have time alone with Caitlyn.

"I don't want you to think I gave you this position because we are dating, you are damn good at what you do, it deserves more praise than I can give" I told her, and she began to cry again, I walked up to her and wiped her tears away.

"You're doing a good job at praising me, this promotion means everything to me, thank you and I would never expect special treatment, mostly" she said and laughed at her own joke making me laugh too.

"Only when it counts, like tonight, would you like to come over for dinner and to spend the night? Sasha and Darcy are going to Persephone's to meet, and I trust them to not start a world war" I asked her as I held her hands and she smiled so big it reached her eyes.

"I'd love that" she agreed, I leaned in for a kiss, then another and quickly stopped myself before we were caught. Then we headed back to the office to order lunch since Persephone was joining us.

We spent the rest of the day working with Caitlyn to discuss what was to happen and it was nothing new she had to learn but she had to work a different way than what she was used to. There were different aspects like marketing and purchases, but she would get the grasp of it very quickly. When it was time to leave I told her to be at mine at 7pm and then we went our separate ways. I had to kick out Sasha and Darcy, get the house cleaned up and begin to start cooking.

I wore a simple outfit consisting of jeans and a white T-shirt and on the menu for tonight was paprika chicken with rice and then for dessert was the cliché of chocolate covered strawberries. I was adding the finishing touches to the meal when I heard a knock at the door and I ran towards it opening it to see Caitlyn copying me with a casual outfit, as she wore cuffed jeans, a light blue blouse, and her hair tousled to one side.

"Hey beautiful, come in" I greeted her and placed a kiss on her cheek as she entered, I led her to the kitchen as she inhaled the scent of spices.

"This smells divine, did you really cook all this?" she asked, and I led her to the dining table and pulled out her chair disappearing shortly only to come back with two plates full of what I had prepared and then poured us each a glass of white wine. She saw the food then took her first bite and I tried to push the thoughts coming into my head by what I heard but I was happy she liked it.

"So, what do you think?" I asked already knowing the answer as I sipped my wine then I smirked at her as she gave me a look knowing the answer.

"I think I just made love with chicken, River this is truly delicious" she complimented, and I thanked her.

"Just wait till dessert" I teased and then took my first bite, and I did do a good job on this.

"Who taught you how to cook?" she asked to make light conversation.

"My grandma, I used to go to her house every weekend and she'd teach me basic cooking and baking skills and when I was 13 she gave me my first cookbook. I've just loved it ever since. It's nice watching people try something you made and seeing their reaction" I told her, and she smiled at how I talked about my past.

"That's cute, I wish I had that. I'm proud when I don't burn a piece of bread in the toaster" she joked, and I laughed along with her.

"I'll teach you how to set the toaster just right" I added on, and she shook her head but enjoyed the banter we had.

We finished up the meal and had a couple of the strawberries but were very full of the chicken, so we didn't eat too many. After I put the dishes into the sink to deal with later, I led her through the house for a tour and ended with my bedroom and became nervous like a teenager inviting their girlfriend over for the first time. She walked around my room looking at photo frames I had and the books I kept on my shelf.

"Can I ask you something?" she looked to me as I sat on the edge of my bed, I gave her a nod to continue. "What was your last relationship like?" she asked, and I scoffed and laughed at that.

"What makes you think I've dated before?" I asked her and she looked at me with disbelief.

"I don't believe that" she said and came to sit next to me.

"It wasn't good, so I don't talk about it" I said, and she held my hand and I remembered that she told me about her past which was worse than mine, so I thought it was time to finally open up to her. "It was 13 years ago, she used me and stole from me, treated me as a bank, just taking everything. After that relationship, I closed myself off, put up so many walls and didn't reveal as much as I wanted but you tried and got through to me. You are different, you see me for me, and I appreciate that so much" I told her and leaned in to place a kiss on her cheek but she turned her face at the last second so I met her lips.

"Show me how much you appreciate me" she teased against my lips, and I pulled back to look into her eyes to see a darker shade was now present.

"Are you sure?" I asked and she answered by pulling me into another kiss.

I laid her down on the bed as I continued to kiss her and unbuttoned her blouse at the same time. As I opened it I trailed the kisses to her neck then down her chest, her stomach and then worked my way back up to remove her blouse and bra then took my time worshipping her body.

I let my hand caress her breast as my mouth gave attention to the other and then switching with ease, each time a gasp escaped her lips or her back arched let me know I was doing the right thing. She reached around my neck and brought me into a kiss then took off my shirt leaving me in my chest binder which I quickly removed to let our bodies press against one another letting the warmth be felt by each other.

I kissed her again and let my hand move down her body to her jeans as I undid the button and unzipped them slowly she switched our positions, so I was now on my back, and she mimicked my actions doing the same. We both kicked ourselves out of our jeans and removed our underwear and took time to take in each other's body.

She was the first to claim me as she pinned me down and took a more dominant position, but she had yet to see what I can do for her. She kissed down my body but not going too far as she returned to my neck and let her fingers glide down my body to where I ached the most for her touch.

Her fingers penetrated me where I needed it most as my hand gripped her forearm that did the work and guided her to where the nerves were sensitive. My back arched as my other hand gripped the bed sheets beneath me turning my knuckles white and my toes curled as I felt her fingers work their magic. A final twist of her fingers and I succumbed to her touch as my breathes evened out and I finally opened my eyes to see her above me and brought her into a kiss just to switch positions to give her the same pleasure.

Instead of using my fingers I went for the more oral approach, I kissed down her body as I reached up and let my hands intertwine with hers. I reached her thighs and teased the inner parts just coaxing over where she needed it.

"River, please" she begged as a moan escaped her lips, I let my lips and tongue work their way through her core. Her back arched and I held her hips down to keep the pace I was going as her hand reached down to grip my hair tight making me work harder for the satisfaction I was aiming to give her. As I found her most sensitive spot she let the bliss fill her as I helped her ride out her orgasm and then kissed back up her body as she was getting her breath back. I kissed her chin, her forehead and then her lips letting myself linger for a moment to savour this like it would be our last.

We got under the sheets, and I wrapped my arm around her as she snuggled against my side. The silence was comfortable as we both knew what the other was thinking and hoped for more of these peaceful and special moments. I kissed her head as she held my free hand with hers.

"You okay?" I whispered to her after I heard her breath slow down.

"I'm great, you?" she asked and looked up at me. I gripped her chin and kissed her again.

"Perfect" I said, and we spent the night cuddled up and falling asleep in each other's arms.

Chapter Fifteen

CAITLYN

A year later

It had been a whole year since everything had happened and a lot had changed. The company was at the peak of all industries, it was the highest it has ever been in profits due to bringing in the department of real estate and with the connections in Italy, Black Corp was starting to expand into the European circuit in addition to the US. Soon it would be a name known worldwide.

As for my work, I have the best job, working beside River and Persephone as the COO but it was too much to take care of their needs as assistant as well so I had to hold back on that and instead opted to get an assistant for each of us and it worked like a well-oiled machine.

As for River's family, Persephone was getting better at opening up about her past to her sisters whenever questions or situations came up. I never found out what had happened with Reginald, but as long as it wasn't part of my life I was content. She and Luiza decided to stay in California to restart their lives properly here, I heard Luiza was trying to open her own gallery since she had an artistic eye, and it would be an easier job with her background.

River and I were closer than ever, and it eventually came out within the company that we were dating by getting caught accidentally. No one really cared, they knew River wasn't like the former manager and if they did have a problem, Persephone would have dealt with them as everyone still feared her. River would spend most nights at mine since at her home she had Darcy and her best friend so after six months of going back and forth I just asked her to move in. She was reluctant at first and didn't want to leave Darcy but knowing she was in the capable hands of Sasha she finally moved in with me, but she still spent some nights there to make sure her sister was doing fine.

Darcy and Persephone did meet on the night we first spent together, and it was awkward for them at first getting to know each other all over again but as the weeks went by and turned into months, they called each other every day. In addition to them working it out, every Sunday the three sisters met up to spend time together getting things back to the way they were always meant to be.

I had River meet my parents after a couple of months and they were shocked by the age gap, but I told them I knew what I was getting myself into and that I was old enough to make my own choices. Despite their first doubts they hit it off really well and were happy that River had a great job that offered opportunities all around including to myself.

I was daydreaming about the year's events as I remembered where I was, I was meeting Persephone for lunch and I was being driven there, I still wasn't used to that. As we finally parked outside the little quaint café, I got out of the car and looked up at the bold sign that read 'Delicate Bites Café' it had been a new addition that became the best and most distinguished location in our small town, after all we had had the project for it and only hired the best. I walked in and spotted Persephone at once walking over to sit with her I could tell she didn't like my ideal place for lunch.

"I would pay you next time to choose anywhere else" she whined but I was now used to how she was. She wasn't as intimidating anymore, she had her moments that still made me rethink my entire being but I got used to her quite easily.

"It's quaint and a favourite, just shut up and enjoy the vibe" I teased, and she shook her head but as the waitress came over we ordered and then grabbed our tablets to speak about the next project we had upcoming.

"Now I have this project that is a shot in the dark" Persephone began as I pulled up my list of departments as I sipped my coffee.

"Which department are we looking at?" I asked her and she was silent as I looked up and could tell she was holding something back. "Seph?" I questioned and she quickly responded.

"Look, Remy has a cousin who wants to open her own garage and she's good at what she does and this town could use one, I've seen the amount of traffic and heard the complaints about going to the next town for repairs, this could be a good investment for us" she told me and it would solve a lot of problems but this would be opening another branch and we already have so many.

"We can arrange a meeting and talk about it, but it doesn't mean it will work" I told her, she bit her lip, and I knew I was missing something, "You didn't?" I questioned but she pointed and as I waited for this mystery person to come over I prepared myself.

I looked to my left to see a handsome woman appear, she seemed to be the same age as myself, she had a muscular build which you could tell by the tank top she wore with ripped jeans. She had dark grey eyes, a matching slit in the eyebrow that I remembered Remy having and had a short undercut hairstyle. Her features were more defined looking masculine with a sharp square jawline and chin.

"Caitlyn this is Nico Costanzo" Persephone introduced, and I shook her hand as she held it out to me.

"Ciao, it's a pleasure to meet you" she said, and the accent was thicker than when I spoke to Remy, she must have spent her life in Italy.

"Likewise so I'm just going to cut to the chase, tell me what you can offer us?" I asked and she began to list her qualities as a mechanic and also mentioned that she can fix up and repair broken down cars and restore them to what they once were. I was impressed with her skills, it wasn't enough but I was a fan of taking risks so I agreed to this project. I told her it would take around three months to build the sort of place she wanted and getting it all approved, but she was fine with waiting. I left them both to talk about the garage more and to probably catch up. Before I left I paid for the bill as my treat, and I was surprised to see the co-manager here.

"Maverick, it's been a while" I said as I paid and I looked at the other woman, she was younger than me by six years, so it was easy to make conversation with her. She had olive skin that complimented her shoulder length black hair and dark eyes, a slim figure and matching my height.

"Who are your friends?" she asked as she nodded to where I just was.

"Oh, I guess my sister-in-law and a cousin of a friend" I said pointing them out and was taken aback by calling Persephone that but maybe one day River and I will get married.

"It seemed important" she said, and I leaned in closer to her.

"Sort of but who knows where it will lead" I told her and she gave me a knowing nod, as I have cancelled projects just as fast before.

"Both attractive but I can see they hold a dark and troubled side, and I don't mess with that" Maverick said, and I looked back at the two women and then back to her.

"Well one is married and the other, I have no idea, but it'll be fun to find out right" I said and took two coffees to go and bid her farewell.

We renovated the company building as well as moving where the head of departments were to the other side of the same floor since there was a huge space we didn't use and extended the office to also fit myself in there and a separate working space for our assistants.

I walked into our office to see River working away, as she looked up, her tired state brightened as she got up and walked over to me. I placed the coffees down and she pulled me into a kiss.

"I'm so glad to see you, save me from work" she complained, and I patted her arm then I placed my things on the desk.

"I have my own work, I'm not here to distract you" I said and leaned on my desk as she joined me, and we looked out of the large window to look at the city.

We stood like this in silence for a moment just enjoying the peaceful moment before we had to get back to work again. I leaned my head on her shoulder as she looked down to me with a content look.

"Who knew we'd end up like this" she said, and I lifted my head and hummed in agreement.

"And there's still so much work to do" I said, and she groaned as we resumed our work to whatever the future holds for us.

Acknowledgements

This book is my first and by no means the last. It means everything to me. I wanted to create something within one of my favourite genres to share it with readers who like stories just like me. I would like to say thank you to everyone who partook in this book to make it what it is.

I would also like to thank everyone in my personal life as they helped me to keep going and pushed me to my limits to keep writing and to not give up when it got difficult.

And also to my family and friends. They encouraged me to keep chasing my dreams.

About the Author

Born in the United Kingdom, Molly discovered a passion for storytelling through countless adventures in Dungeons & Dragons' games. Fuelled by a desire to share their creativity, they pursued two years of college education in game design and although they didn't complete their education in the subject, Molly continues to draw inspiration from the communities they've been a part of. With no formal training in writing, they bring a fresh, imaginative perspective to their work, aiming to captivate readers with the same sense of wonder and excitement that first inspired them.

Milton Keynes UK
Ingram Content Group UK Ltd.
UKHW041514061024
449294UK00013B/175/J

9 781779 621146